KNIVES AT NIGHT

go saw starlight glitter on an upraised blade and
elt the fiery kiss of the knife as it scraped along
eek. He jerked his head aside just in time for
wnward thrust to miss him. His fingers closed
on the greasy buckskins the Paiute wore, and shoved
the man away for a second.

That was long enough for Fargo to reach down to
his calf and slip the Arkansas toothpick from the
fringed sheath strapped there. He brought the heavy
blade up into the Indian's body, feeling it penetrate
deeply. The Paiute grunted in pain. Fargo ripped the
razor-sharp blade across the man's belly, and hot guts
spilled out over his hand. He yanked the knife free,
and pushed the corpse away. . . .

THE TRAILSMAN

#302

BLACK ROCK PASS

by

Jon Sharpe

Ⓢ

A SIGNET BOOK

SIGNET
Published by New American Library, a division of
Penguin Group (USA) Inc., 375 Hudson Street,
New York, New York 10014, USA
Penguin Group (Canada), 90 Eglinton Avenue East, Suite 700, Toronto,
Ontario M4P 2Y3, Canada (a division of Pearson Penguin Canada Inc.)
Penguin Books Ltd., 80 Strand, London WC2R 0RL, England
Penguin Ireland, 25 St. Stephen's Green, Dublin 2,
Ireland (a division of Penguin Books Ltd.)
Penguin Group (Australia), 250 Camberwell Road, Camberwell, Victoria 3124,
Australia (a division of Pearson Australia Group Pty. Ltd.)
Penguin Books India Pvt. Ltd., 11 Community Centre, Panchsheel Park,
New Delhi - 110 017, India
Penguin Group (NZ), cnr Airborne and Rosedale Roads, Albany,
Auckland 1310, New Zealand (a division of Pearson New Zealand Ltd.)
Penguin Books (South Africa) (Pty.) Ltd., 24 Sturdee Avenue,
Rosebank, Johannesburg 2196, South Africa

Penguin Books Ltd., Registered Offices:
80 Strand, London WC2R 0RL, England

First published by Signet, an imprint of New American Library,
a division of Penguin Group (USA) Inc.

First Printing, December 2006
10 9 8 7 6 5 4 3 2 1

The first chapter of this book previously appeared in *High Plains Grifters,*
the three hundred and first volume in this series.

Copyright © Penguin Group (USA) Inc., 2006
All rights reserved

 REGISTERED TRADEMARK—MARCA REGISTRADA

Printed in the United States of America

PUBLISHER'S NOTE
This is a work of fiction. Names, characters, places, and incidents either are
the product of the author's imagination or are used fictitiously, and any resem-
blance to actual persons, living or dead, events, or locales is entirely
coincidental.
   The publisher does not have any control over and does not assume any
responsibility for author or third-party Web sites or their content.

The Trailsman

Beginnings . . . they bend the tree and they mark the man. Skye Fargo was born when he was eighteen. Terror was his midwife, vengeance his first cry. Killing spawned Skye Fargo, ruthless, cold-blooded murder. Out of the acrid smoke of gunpowder still hanging in the air, he rose, cried out a promise never forgotten.

The Trailsman they began to call him all across the West: searcher, scout, hunter, the man who could see where others only looked, his skills for hire but not his soul, the man who lived each day to the fullest, yet trailed each tomorrow. Skye Fargo, the Trailsman, the seeker who could take the wildness of a land and the wanting of a woman and make them his own.

Utah Territory, 1860—
where the Pony Express has linked one side
of the continent with the other,
but the only way to bridge the gap
between good men and bad is with hot lead.

1

The sound of gunfire made the lake blue eyes of the big man in buckskins narrow with suspicion. In this rugged land through which he rode on the magnificent black-and-white Ovaro, a sudden outbreak of shots was almost never a good thing.

Skye Fargo reined the stallion to a halt. He was about halfway up a ridge dotted with scrubby juniper trees, and the gunfire came from somewhere on the other side. Fargo wasn't the sort of man who ran from trouble, so as soon as he had pulled the Henry rifle from its saddle sheath, he heeled the Ovaro into motion again and rode quickly to the top of the slope.

He stopped again there to take stock of the situation. The ridge fell away before him to a broad, flat stretch of semiarid land. A lone man on horseback was galloping from east to west along there, twisting in the saddle from time to time to trigger more shots at a knot of riders about fifty yards behind him.

The pursuers rode ugly little ponies that were faster than they looked like they ought to be. They wore buckskins, feathers, and war paint.

Fargo's jaw tightened as he recognized the Indians as Paiute warriors. The Paiutes had gotten along peacefully with the settlers at times in the past, but like most of the tribes they had eventually gotten tired of the white man's ways and become more warlike.

These Paiutes were doing their damnedest to catch that lone rider, and if they did, what they had in mind for him probably wouldn't be too pleasant.

Down below on the plain, the fleeing man must have emptied the pistol in his hand, because he jammed it back in a holster and drew another revolver from his saddlebags. He turned to fire. His shots weren't doing any good, though. The Paiutes never slowed down.

Fargo lifted the Henry to his shoulder. The distance was about three hundred yards, not an easy shot, but not too difficult, either, at least not for him. He aimed, held his breath, and squeezed the trigger.

The pony ridden by the warrior who was in the lead stumbled and then collapsed as Fargo's bullet struck it in the chest. Fargo hated having to kill the horse, but the alternative was to shoot the Indian, and he wanted to do that even less.

While the echoes of the first shot were still rolling over the landscape, Fargo worked the rifle's lever, shifted his aim, and fired again. A second horse went down, tossing its rider over its head. The Paiute flew through the air and crashed to the ground not far from where the first warrior had fallen when Fargo shot his horse out from under him.

The other three Indians began pulling back, unsure where the shots were coming from. One of the two who had been unhorsed ran after them, but the other warrior snatched up the rifle he had dropped when he fell. He lifted it and drew a bead on the still-fleeing rider.

Fargo said, "Damn," and jacked another round into the Henry's chamber. He hadn't figured on the Paiute being so blasted stubborn. He fired, but not in time to keep the warrior from pulling the trigger, too. Smoke geysered from the muzzle of the Paiute's rifle.

An instant later Fargo's bullet struck him and lifted him off his feet, throwing him backward. The warrior landed with arms and legs flopping in the boneless sprawl that signified death.

At the same time, the rider jerked in the saddle and sagged forward, but managed to hang on and keep riding. Fargo knew that the Paiute's final shot had struck the man. That last-ditch effort had found its target.

He turned to look at the rest of the war party. One of them had picked up the other man Fargo had set afoot, and now they were riding double. Dust boiled up from the hooves of the horses as the Paiutes took off for the tall and uncut. Obviously, they didn't want any part of the deadly accurate rifleman on top of the ridge.

Fargo lowered the Henry and then replaced it in the saddle sheath. He looked at the lone rider and saw that the man had slowed his horse to a trot. Whether or not that was deliberate, Fargo didn't know. He heeled the Ovaro into motion again and headed down the slope toward the wounded man.

The rider's horse came to a complete stop before Fargo could get there. The man swayed back and forth a couple of times and then pitched out of the saddle to fall heavily to the ground.

Fargo urged the stallion to a faster gait. By the time he reached the wounded man, the hombre's horse had wandered off a short distance and started cropping at the sparse grass. The man hadn't moved since he fell.

Fargo swung down quickly from the saddle and dropped to a knee beside the man, who lay facedown. Keeping one eye peeled for the Paiute war party, just in case the Indians decided to double back, Fargo carefully rolled the man over.

He was more of a kid than a man, Fargo saw, probably no more than seventeen or eighteen years old. Lank blond hair fell around a thin face. He wore buckskin trousers and a homespun shirt, and both back and front of that shirt were stained with blood. Fate had guided that hastily fired bullet clean through him.

Fargo figured the youngster didn't have more than a few minutes to live. Anger made his jaw with its close-cropped dark beard clench hard. Violent death was always part of the frontier and was never far away, but it made Fargo mad when the victim was someone this young.

The youngster's eyelids flickered open. He stared up at Fargo without really seeming to see him at first. A thin line of blood trickled from the corner of his mouth. When his eyes finally focused, he asked hoarsely, "How . . . how bad . . . am I hurt?"

"Pretty bad, son," Fargo said as gently as he could. He started to stand up.

"D-don't go!" the youngster said desperately.

"Just getting my canteen," Fargo told him. "A drink of water might make you feel a little better." And it might ease the young man's passing, Fargo thought.

He fetched the canteen that hung from the Ovaro's saddle and then knelt beside the wounded man again, getting an arm around his shoulders and lifting him a little. Fargo propped the youngster against his knee and held the mouth of the canteen to his lips. The young man sucked thirstily on it for a moment and then said, "Yeah . . . yeah, that's good. . . ."

"What's your name?" Fargo asked.

"B-Billy . . . Conners. I ride for . . . the Pony Express."

Fargo frowned. He wasn't too surprised by what Billy Conners had just told him. He knew that most of the riders for the recently established Pony Express were young men. "Orphans Preferred," in fact, was the way Russell, Majors, and Waddell, the people who started the mail delivery service, had advertised for employees. The company hired young, slender men whose weight wouldn't slow down the horses they rode. Billy Conners fit that description.

"I reckon that's a mail pouch on your horse," Fargo said.

"Y-yeah. Mister, I . . . I hate to ask it . . . but can you see the pouch through? Get it where it's . . . goin'?"

"Where's that?" Fargo asked.

"Next relay station is . . . Black Rock Pass . . . 'bout five miles . . . west o' here."

Fargo didn't hesitate. He nodded and said, "Yeah, Billy. I'll get the mail pouch to the station at Black Rock Pass. That is, if you can't deliver it yourself."

Despite the lines of pain etched on his face, a grim smile tugged at the corners of Billy Conners' mouth. "You ain't . . . much of a liar . . . mister. I know I . . . ain't gonna make it. That's why I 'preciate you . . . makin' sure the mail gets through."

"Rest easy on that score," Fargo assured him. "It'll get there."

Billy licked his lips, and Fargo gave him a little more water. The drink made him cough this time, and quite a bit of blood came up, flecking his chin and the front of his shirt. When the coughing spell passed, the youngster said, "Them damn Paiutes . . . come out of nowhere to jump me. I was . . . bein' careful. I've . . . rode this route . . . before."

"Sometimes it doesn't matter how careful you are," Fargo told him. "Things still catch up to you."

"Y-yeah." Billy blinked several times, and the life seemed to fade some in his brown eyes. But it hadn't gone out of them completely, and he forced himself to say, "M-mister . . . who are you?"

"My name's Skye Fargo."

Billy's eyes widened a little with pain or recognition or both. "F-Fargo . . ." he said. "Imagine th-that." He began to shake as if with a chill. "I get myself shot . . . and who comes along . . . to help me . . . but the Trailsman!"

A sudden, sharply indrawn breath hissed between his teeth, and his back arched a little. When the air came out of him with a sigh, the rest of Billy Conners' life came with it. A glassy haze settled over his unseeing eyes. Grimly, Fargo closed them.

Then he eased Billy's body to the ground and stood up. He had a promise to keep. He walked toward Billy's horse, talking quietly to it.

The animal started to shy away, and Fargo noticed that it was favoring one leg. That explained why the Indian ponies had been able to keep up. Normally the grain-fed mounts used by the Pony Express could outrun the grass-fed Indian ponies. Even though this horse hadn't yet gone lame, it wasn't able to run at full speed.

Fargo's soothing tones calmed the animal enough so that he was able to catch hold of its reins. Once the horse felt Fargo's hand on the reins it settled down even more. He unhooked the mail pouch that was strapped to the saddle and carried it over to the Ovaro, where he fastened it to his own saddle.

Then Fargo lifted Billy's body and carefully draped it over the back of the Pony Express horse. The youngster's light weight made it easy for Fargo to handle him. The smell of blood made the mount a little nervous again, but Fargo got the corpse tied in place.

He swung up onto the stallion and rode west, leading the Pony Express mount with its grim burden. A range of small, rounded peaks rose in front of him. Fargo had been through these parts before and knew they were called the Cricket Range. Black Rock Pass led through the mountains, and beyond it was desert that stretched to the Nevada border. Fargo hadn't known that a Pony Express relay station had been established at the pass, but he wasn't surprised.

Keeping an eye on his back-trail, he pushed on through the afternoon, leaving the flats and riding through increasingly rugged terrain. He saw no sign of the Paiutes following him, but that didn't mean they weren't back there. They would be unlikely to forget that he had killed one of the warriors and two horses. And they might have been part of an even larger band that was raiding through this southwestern corner of Utah Territory.

For a man like Fargo, whose keen eyes saw things that another man's might not have, the trail used by the Pony Express riders was easy to follow. It led him on a winding path through the mountains before emerging onto a long, straight, gradually declining slope. At the bottom of that slope, on the dividing line between mountains and desert, stood a couple of buildings. Fargo knew that had to be the location of the Black Rock Pass relay station.

The sun was a red ball not far above the horizon as he rode down the trail toward the station. He saw horses moving around in the corral behind a barn made of roughly sawn planks, and a couple of large tan-and-brown dogs barked at him from the porch of a large building made of stone and logs.

He didn't see any people, though, and that made him frown slightly. It was too early for everybody to have turned in; someone should have been out and about.

No sooner had that thought gone through Fargo's mind than a rifle boomed and he heard the high whine of a bullet passing somewhere over his head. He reined in sharply, debating whether to pile out of the saddle and hunt some cover.

He decided not to, because the slug hadn't really come that close. His instincts told him it had been a warning shot. He waited to see what was going to happen next.

The barn was about fifty yards away, the other building some twenty yards beyond that. The voice that hailed Fargo a moment later came from the barn.

"Who are you, mister, and what do you want here?"

The voice was rough and gravelly, the voice of a man tough enough to live here at this isolated relay station where there was always the danger of Indian attacks, bad weather, and roaming desperadoes. It didn't really sound hostile, though, just cautious.

"Is this the Black Rock Pass Pony Express station?" Fargo called back. "If it is, I've got one of your riders here."

He moved the Ovaro aside so that the man hidden in the barn could get a better view of the other horse with the body draped over its saddle. Fargo heard a startled, profane exclamation, and then the man yelled, "If you killed him, damn you—"

Fargo held up his hands to forestall the inevitable threat. "I didn't kill him," he said in loud, clear tones. "A Paiute warrior did. I came across him being chased by five of them and tried to give him a hand, but one of the Indians got off a lucky shot." He lowered one hand and pointed to the canvas bag hanging from his saddle. "I've got the mail pouch here, too."

There was a moment of silence from the barn, and then the man called, "Come ahead. But if this is some kind o' trick, I'll blow a hole clean through you, mister."

"No trick," Fargo assured the man as he hitched the Ovaro into a walk and trailed the other horse behind him.

As he approached the barn, a man stepped out and trained a Sharps rifle on him. The man was short and muscular, with very broad shoulders. He wore a battered old hat with the brim turned up. The hat was crammed down on a thatch of rusty hair. A mustache of the same shade drooped around the man's mouth.

"That's far enough," he called when Fargo was about twenty feet away. "Now step down from that horse and keep your hands where I can see 'em."

Fargo did as the man said, figuring it would be easier to cooperate than to argue. He stepped aside without being told to and said, "I'm sorry about your rider getting killed. He lived for a few minutes after I reached him. He told me his name and asked me to see that the mail pouch got here as scheduled."

"Well, it ain't exactly as scheduled," the man rumbled. "We was expectin' him an hour ago. What was his name?"

Fargo figured the question was a test, to see if he was telling the truth. "Billy Conners."

The man grunted. "Yeah, that's right. I reckon you could've found it out some other way, though."

Fargo's patience was beginning to run out. He said, "Look, you can believe me or not, I don't really care. I told you what happened. Here's the boy's body and the mail pouch. If you don't want me around here, I'll mount up and move on."

"You said an Injun shot him?"

"That's right."

"What happened to the Injun?"

"I killed him," Fargo said. "Just not quite in time to save Billy. I'm sorry about that."

The man finally lowered his Sharps a little. "You know, I believe you are," he said. "What happened to the rest of the war party?"

"They hightailed it after I shot a couple of their horses. I guess they figured killing me would be more trouble than it was worth."

"Yeah, them red devils like to have the odds on

their side." The man lowered the rifle the rest of the way. "You never did tell me your name."

"Skye Fargo."

The bushy red eyebrows went up in surprise. "The Trailsman?"

"Some call me that," Fargo admitted.

"Hell, man, you helped lay out some o' the old stagecoach routes that Russell, Majors, and Waddell are usin' for the Pony Express!"

Fargo shrugged. "That was a while back."

"Sorry I held a gun on you. I didn't know who you were."

"No way you could have," Fargo said.

"I'm Sam Maguire, stationkeeper here," the man introduced himself. He walked past Fargo to look more closely at Billy Conners' body in the rapidly fading light. "Damn shame. Billy was a good boy and a fine rider. If you want to hand me that mail pouch, I'll take it inside. I'd get it myself, but that black-and-white horse of yours looks like he'd take a bite outta my hide if I got too close."

"He just might," Fargo agreed with a faint smile. He took the pouch off the saddle and held it out toward Maguire. "He can be a little touchy around people he doesn't know."

"Thanks," Maguire said as he took the pouch. "There's an empty stall in the barn, and plenty o' grain in the bin and water in the trough. You're welcome to whatever you need."

"Much obliged," Fargo said with a nod.

"You'll be spendin' the night?"

"If that's all right with you."

"Sure," Maguire said. He grinned. "This far out in the middle o' nowhere, a fella's got to be hospitable if he ever wants to have any company besides rattle-snakes and Paiutes . . . and I ain't sure which o' those is worse!"

Fargo wondered who was going to carry the mail pouch on the next leg of its journey. He knew that the Pony Express riders sometimes laid over at relay stations like this, so there might be one of them inside the building. If not, the mail might have to wait until the next rider came through. The superintendent of this section wouldn't like that, and neither would the bosses back east, but sometimes a little trouble couldn't be avoided.

Instead of asking about the mail, Fargo said, "I suppose you'll bury him."

Maguire took the reins of Billy's horse. "Sure will. First thing in the mornin'. It'll take a while to dig a grave since the ground's so hard hereabouts, but I'm always up early anyway."

"I'll give you a hand," Fargo offered as they led the two horses into the barn.

"Now it's me who's much obliged. But I've got help, so there shouldn't be any need."

Fargo hadn't seen anyone else around the place, but Maguire's comment sure made it sound like he wasn't alone here. Fargo waited for the stationkeeper to go on, but Maguire didn't say anything else. He untied Billy's body from the saddle and carefully lowered it to the ground, onto a sheet of canvas that he spread out first. Fargo helped him roll the body into the canvas.

Maguire lashed the bundle closed with some rawhide thongs and said, "He'll keep until mornin'. It gets pretty chilly out here at night, even in the spring like this."

Fargo nodded agreement, and Maguire went on, "Come on in the house whenever you've finished tendin' to your horse. Supper ought to be just about ready."

Again, that was an indication that Maguire wasn't alone here. Otherwise, who had fixed the supper?

Fargo figured he would find out soon enough. By the time he had unsaddled and rubbed down the Ovaro, then made sure the stallion had plenty of grain and water, the sun was completely down and night was falling fast, the way it did in these parts. As he walked toward the other building, he saw yellow light glowing warmly in its windows.

The dogs barked ferociously as Fargo climbed the steps to the porch, but their tails were wagging and he knew the barking was just for show. Sure enough, both of the big curs crowded around him, sniffing him happily and licking his hands. He roughed up the fur on top of their heads and rubbed their floppy ears.

The door opened, letting out more of the light so that it slanted across the porch. "Just kick them damn dogs outta the way," Sam Maguire rumbled as he bulked in the doorway. "Mutts're always underfoot, more trouble than they're worth."

From behind him, a female voice admonished, "Pa! Don't talk that way about the dogs. And don't tell people to kick them, either!"

The presence of a woman—and from the sound of her voice, a young one—here at the relay station surprised Fargo. He thought that life here would be an awfully lonely existence, and that was hard on a woman. Men seemed to bear up better under the solitude of frontier life.

But that wasn't always true, and this woman sounded feisty, like she had a lot of spirit. That would help her endure the harsh, difficult conditions.

Maguire ignored the woman and said, "Come on in, Fargo. Stew's ready."

Fargo had already smelled the delicious aroma. He stepped into the house and found himself in a large room that served as parlor, dining room, and kitchen, all in one. There were a couple of rocking chairs and a few cane-bottomed chairs over by a fireplace with a stone mantel, a long table flanked by benches, a big cast-iron stove, rugs made from the hides of various animals on the floor, and several sets of antelope antlers mounted on the wall. Nothing fancy, but the place had an air of being comfortable about it.

And it was full of people, which also took Fargo by surprise. Maguire wasn't even close to being alone here.

Two little boys came running over to stare up at Fargo. They were about eight years old, with identical freckled faces and red hair that stuck straight up. A boy of about sixteen came across the room, too, at a more deliberate pace than the twins but with just as much interest directed toward the stranger in buckskins.

A woman stood at the stove, stirring a pot of stew. A few silver streaks in her brown hair put her in middle age. Maguire's wife and the mother of the three boys, Fargo guessed. But she *wasn't* the one who had called out a minute earlier.

The owner of that voice stood near the stove, too, and although her gaze was more discreet than those of her brothers, she was no less interested in Fargo. She was the oldest of the youngsters, nineteen or maybe even twenty. Thick red hair tumbled around her face and over her shoulders, falling most of the way down her back, Fargo saw as she blushed a little and half turned away.

Not before he caught a glimpse of compelling green eyes, though.

There was one more person in the room, a man who sat at the table with cards spread out in a solitaire hand in front of him. Even though the man was sitting, Fargo could tell that he was tall. He wore a dusty black suit and a broad-brimmed hat. A string tie was cinched around his neck, and Fargo caught a glimpse of a fancy vest under the dark coat. The man's face was long and slender and made to seem even more so by the pointed goatee he wore. He glanced at Fargo with a hint of a mocking smile on his thin lips.

Fargo instinctively disliked the man on sight, and he had a hunch that the feeling was mutual.

"Welcome," Maguire said as he ushered Fargo in. "It ain't much, but it's home."

"For now," the redheaded girl said. "Until the Paiutes come in the dead of night and kill us all in our beds."

2

Maguire turned to scowl at her for a second, then said to Fargo, "You'll have to forgive my daughter. She has the Irish flare for the dramatic, even when there's nothin' to what she's sayin'."

"Nothing?" the girl shot back. "They killed Billy Conners. And how many stations have they attacked along the route? How many men have they killed in other places?"

"We can handle a little Indian trouble," Maguire insisted.

"It's not a little Indian trouble. It's an Indian war."

One of the twins looked up at Maguire and asked, "Are the Injuns gonna scalp us, Pa?"

"I need my scalp," the other one said.

Maguire said, "I pity the Paiute who tries to mess with a couple o' little hellions like you two. You'd send him runnin' back straight to his lodge, wouldn't you?"

"We would if we had guns."

"Yeah, can we have guns?"

"No guns," said the woman at the stove as she began to ladle the stew into wooden bowls. "You'd come a lot closer to shooting each other than you would to shooting a Paiute."

"Introductions are in order," Maguire said. "Mr.

Fargo, the lady at the stove is my wife Ava. These two rapscallions"—he ruffled the hair of the little boys, much as Fargo had with the dogs—"are Matthew and Patrick. The older boy there is my son Terence, and the girl who thinks we're all going to be massacred in our beds is my daughter Colleen."

Fargo took his hat off, caught Ava Maguire's eye, and nodded politely to her. "I'm honored to be in your home, ma'am," he said, "and to meet you and your children."

"You're welcome, sir. We never turn away visitors." Ava glanced pointedly toward the man at the table, who seemingly paid little attention to what was going on around him. Fargo would have been willing to bet that the gent didn't miss much, though.

Maguire stepped closer to the table and said, "And this is Mr. Porter, another visitor who rode in earlier today."

The man glanced up at Fargo again but didn't offer his hand. He murmured, "William Henry Porter, at your service, sir."

"Skye Fargo," the Trailsman introduced himself. He didn't offer to shake hands, either.

"I've heard of you, Mr. Fargo," Terence Maguire said. "You've been a guide and a scout for the army, haven't you?"

Fargo nodded. "At times, and among other things."

"I've heard nobody knows the frontier better than you."

"I can find my way around," Fargo said. "I don't figure you could ever determine who actually knows the frontier the best, though."

Colleen carried one of the bowls over to the table from the stove. "Here you are, Mr. Fargo," she said. "Sit down and enjoy your supper."

As she placed the bowl on the table, she bent over and Fargo got an intriguing glimpse of the valley between her breasts when the neckline of her dress dropped away from them for a second. She was a well-built young woman, with her breasts high and firm and her hips possessing sensuous curves below a trim waist. Fargo didn't stare, though. It wouldn't have been very proper to accept a man's hospitality and then leer at his daughter.

He sat down on the bench, on the opposite side of the table from William Henry Porter, who began gathering up his cards and putting them away inside his coat. Porter had the look of a gambler about him. Fargo wondered what such a man was doing out here, far from the towns and the saloons that would hold the suckers necessary for Porter to make his living.

Colleen and her mother brought more bowls of stew to the table, and soon everyone was sitting down and eating. The stew had chunks of salted beef in it, along with savory wild onions and pieces of carrots and potatoes. Fargo thought it was very good. It sure beat gnawing on jerky while in the saddle. Too many of his meals lately had been like that.

As they ate, Maguire asked, "Where are you bound, Mr. Fargo, if you don't mind me inquirin'?"

"California, eventually," Fargo replied. "I'm taking my time about getting there, though. I'm supposed to meet a man in San Francisco the last week in June."

"That's more than a month and a half off. You ought to make it, even without hurrying."

"That's what I thought. I haven't been through these parts in a while, so I thought I'd take a good look at the country along the way."

"You picked a bad time. The Paiutes *are* up in arms, although I wouldn't call it a war." Maguire looked at his daughter as he added that last comment.

"I hadn't seen any hostiles until today."

"You were lucky. There have been several instances of trouble in recent weeks. It was a hard winter, and

17

some o' the Paiutes starved and froze to death. For some reason, they blame the whites for that. One o' their chiefs, a fella called Numaga, has been tryin' to talk sense into them, tellin' 'em they don't want to go to war with the white man, but those hotheaded young braves don't listen to him. Especially when they got another chief, Satonga, eggin' 'em on."

Fargo hadn't heard of either of those chiefs, but he wasn't surprised. He had no reason to keep up with who was in charge of the various bands of Paiutes.

"Satonga's bad," one of the twins said. Fargo wasn't sure which one was Matthew and which one was Patrick. It didn't seem to matter, though, since both of them always spoke up.

"If anybody scalps us, it'll be him," the other one said.

"But we could kill him—"

"If we had guns."

"Not until you're older, and then only for hunting," Ava said firmly.

"What are you going to do with that mail pouch?" Fargo asked Maguire. "Wait until the next westbound rider comes through?"

Before Maguire could answer, Terence said, "I'll take it."

Ava looked startled and put down her spoon next to her bowl. "You'll do no such thing," she said. "You're just a boy."

"Billy Conners was only a year older'n me," Terence protested.

"And Billy Conners is dead," his mother pointed out. "Do you want the Indians to get you, too?"

"Aw, Ma . . . I've ridden the route before. You know that."

Ava's lips thinned. "And it was too dangerous then, too. I didn't like it."

"I can outrun any bunch of Indians," Terence insisted. "Their ponies can't keep up with our horses."

"They kept up with Billy's horse," Ava said. "They caught him, remember?"

"Well, to be fair," Maguire said tentatively, "I did notice that Billy's horse has a bum leg. It couldn't run as fast as it usually can."

Fargo could have confirmed that, but he kept his mouth shut except for eating stew. He didn't want to get mixed up in a family quarrel.

"Our horses are all in top-notch shape," Maguire went on. "The boy's probably right. He *could* outrun any of those Injun ponies. And the superintendent will raise holy hell if that mail pouch is a week late."

"Samuel, watch your language," Ava snapped. "Little pitchers."

"What do you mean by that, Ma?" one of the twins asked.

"Just never you mind," she told him. "And Terence, you're not riding the route, not now. That's final."

Terence opened his mouth to argue some more, but his father held up a hand to stop him. Muttering disappointedly under his breath, Terence went back to his stew.

Maguire turned to Fargo. "What about you, Mr. Fargo?" he asked. "Any chance that you could take the pouch? Nobody would expect you to make the time that our riders normally do, but if you could see your way clear to carryin' it . . ."

Fargo thought about it. He had promised the dying Billy Conners that he would bring the mail pouch here to Black Rock Pass, but he hadn't said anything about carrying it farther than that.

But he had pledged that the mail would get through, he reminded himself, and that could be taken in more than one way. He supposed there was a chance he *had* committed himself to toting the pouch on west, until a regular Pony Express rider could take on the responsibility for its delivery.

He was about to say that he would take the pouch with him when he left in the morning, but suddenly the dogs began barking fiercely on the porch. There was something different about the sound this time, something more urgent. Between barks the dogs snarled and growled, as if they were really upset.

"Something's out there," one of the twins said excitedly.

"Or somebody," added the other. Together they said, "Injuns!"

"Sit still," Maguire said. "It's probably just a mountain lion prowlin' around or somethin' like that." He pushed his chair back, its legs scraping on the puncheon floor. "I'll go have a look-see."

"Be careful, Samuel," Ava said worriedly.

Fargo stood up as well and said, "I'll go with you." He looked at Porter, waiting to see if the man would volunteer to join them, but the gambler just stared down into his bowl of stew and made a point of ignoring Fargo's gaze.

With a little shrug and a twist of his mouth, Fargo turned away and walked to the door with Maguire. He had brought his Henry rifle with him when he came in from the barn, and leaned it against the wall next to the door. He picked it up while Maguire was lifting down the Sharps from a pair of hooks on the wall.

"Might be a good idea to blow out the lamps before we step outside," Fargo suggested. "That way we won't be silhouetted against the light while we're in the doorway."

"Yeah, I reckon you're right." Maguire looked at his wife. "Ava . . ."

She was already on her feet, leaning over the lamp that was on the table. "Terence, get the others," she said and then blew out the flame with a puff of breath.

Darkness descended on the big room as the lamps were blown out. Enough starlight came through the windows so that Fargo could see Sam Maguire beside him. He made another suggestion. "As soon as we're outside, the shutters ought to be closed over these windows."

"I was about to say that," Maguire responded. "I ain't a babe in the woods, Fargo."

"Didn't mean to imply that you were. I just want to be sure that your family is as safe as possible."

"Me, too. Terence, Colleen, close the shutters as soon as me and Mr. Fargo are outside. Be ready to bar the door if need be, too."

Ava said, "But then you'd be shut outside, Samuel. We can't—"

"If there's shootin', do it," Maguire said, his voice hard, brooking no argument.

Whether that tone would work on a wife, though, was open to debate, thought Fargo. They would have to just wait and see what happened. Maguire might be right; it might be just a mountain lion or some other wild animal that had spooked the dogs.

The big curs were still barking and growling. The noise grew louder as Maguire swung the door open. He and Fargo moved through it quickly, stepping out onto the porch. Fargo pulled the door closed behind him.

Maguire went to the left along the porch, Fargo to the right. Both men paused. Fargo tried to listen, but it was hard to hear anything over the racket being set up by the dogs. Maguire had the same problem. "Hush, you brutes!" the stationkeeper hissed.

The dogs ignored him and kept barking until Maguire kicked one of them lightly in the rump. That one yelped a little and fell silent, and the other followed suit.

Fargo's eyes searched the starlight-dappled landscape and his ears were keenly attuned to anything out of the ordinary. He heard the yowl of a panther up in the hills overlooking the relay station, probably a half mile or more away.

Maguire heard it, too, and grunted in relief. "Told you it was probably just a big cat got these mongrels stirred up," he said. He started to turn toward the door.

Fargo heard a soft fluttering sound and recognized it for what it was. An instant later, the arrow that came out of the darkness struck Maguire's left arm with a thud, burying its sharp flint head deep in the flesh. Maguire cried out in pain and staggered, dropping the Sharps.

Instinctively, Fargo threw himself to the floor of the porch even as he realized that, by turning away, Maguire had accidentally saved his own life. If the stationkeeper hadn't moved when he did, that arrow would have buried itself in his chest, rather than his upper arm.

Fargo had barely hit the planks when another deadly, feathered missile flew out of the darkness. It cut through the air above him and hit the house, sticking in a log with its shaft quivering. Fargo raised himself on his elbows and lifted the Henry as a couple of shadowy figures rushed toward the porch.

He fired, flame licking from the muzzle of the rifle, and one of the charging Indians was driven backward as if he had just run into a stone wall. The other came on, screeching with hate. The time for stealth was over.

Fargo levered the Henry and fired again, but the Paiute darted aside at just the right instant, warned

22

perhaps by some savage instinct. He leaped at Fargo, bounding high to land on the porch.

Fargo rolled aside, barely avoiding the downward stroke of a war ax. He thrust the rifle up, jamming the barrel hard under the warrior's chin. The man gurgled in pain and staggered back a couple of steps, his hand going to his throat. That gave Fargo enough room to roll again and come up on one knee. He palmed out the revolver on his hip. Colt flame bloomed in the darkness as he fired. The bullet smashed into the Paiute's chest and flung him backward off the porch.

Twisting toward Sam Maguire, Fargo saw that the stationkeeper had fallen to his knees. Maguire managed to pick up the heavy rifle he had dropped, though, and as more of the Paiutes charged the house, he was able to lift it and pull the trigger. The Sharps boomed. One of the Indians flipped over in a backward somersault as the .52 caliber slug blew a hole the size of a fist through him.

Fargo fired twice more, the Colt bucking against his palm as it blasted, and he saw another of the attackers go spinning off his feet. But then a Paiute came around the corner of the house and tackled Fargo from the side, crashing into him and knocking him flat on the porch. The revolver slipped out of his fingers and slid away across the planks.

Fargo saw starlight glitter on an upraised blade and then felt the fiery kiss of the knife as it scraped along his cheek. He had jerked his head aside just in time for the downward thrust to miss him. His fingers closed on the greasy buckskins the Paiute wore, and he was able to shove the man away for a second.

That was long enough for Fargo to reach down to his calf and slip the Arkansas toothpick from the fringed sheath strapped there. He brought the heavy blade up into the Indian's body, feeling it penetrate deeply. The Paiute grunted in pain. Fargo ripped the razor-sharp blade across the man's belly. Hot guts spilled out over his hand. Fargo yanked the knife free and pushed the corpse away. The Indian had died without another sound.

The door banged open. Terence came onto the porch, a rifle in his hands. He fired at the Indians, and one of them howled in pain. Colleen darted out behind her brother and bent to grab her father's unwounded arm. "Come on, Pa!" she urged. "Get back inside!"

"Damn it, girl!" Maguire yelled. "You were supposed to bar the door!"

"No time for that, Pa. Come on!"

Maguire reeled to his feet with Colleen's help and stumbled toward the door. Meanwhile, Fargo switched the Arkansas toothpick from right hand to left and picked up his Colt again. He emptied the revolver at the Paiutes, who had turned to flee, but he couldn't tell if he hit any of them or not.

"They're runnin'!" Terence cried in triumph.

Fargo holstered the Colt and found his Henry. He sent a couple of shots after the Indians to hurry them on their way. Then he said to Terence, "Back inside!" Maguire and Colleen had already vanished into the house.

Fargo bent to wipe the blood off the toothpick's blade on the buckskins of the man he had killed with the big knife. Then he sheathed it, raised the Henry, and backed into the house, following Terence.

"Is that everyone?" Ava asked, her voice tense with worry as she stood beside the door.

"That's all of us," Fargo told her. Even the dogs were in, having run inside while the door was open. Ava pushed the bar, letting it crash down securely across the door.

"I thought the Injuns were gonna get in the house for sure!" one of the twins said in the thick darkness.

"Did you see the way Terence ran out to fight 'em?" the other one said.

"We could've done that!"

"If we had guns!"

Fargo smiled grimly. Once kids got their minds set on something, they didn't give it up easily, not even in the middle of an Indian attack.

"Better light one of the lamps again," he said. "We'll need to be able to see to get that arrow out of Sam's arm."

Terence asked, "Are the Paiutes gonna come back?"

"More than likely," Fargo replied honestly. "But not for a while. We did too much damage to them. They'll have to think about it and work themselves up again."

A match scratched into life, casting a harsh glare around the room for a moment. Fargo saw that Sam Maguire had found his way to one of the benches beside the table and sunk down on it. His normally ruddy face was ashen from the pain of the arrow in his arm.

Ava hovered over him, an anxious expression on her face. She was clearly unsure of what to do next. Colleen was the one who had struck the match. She held the flame to the wick of the lamp on the table. It caught, and as she lowered the chimney, the glow from it washed out over most of the room.

Fargo saw that the gambler, William Henry Porter, was still sitting at the table, but now there was an ivory-handled pocket pistol lying in front of him, probably taken from a holster under his coat.

"You could have pitched in to help us," Fargo said coolly to him.

Porter shrugged. "I would have . . . if the savages had made it inside."

In other words, he would have tried to defend himself, but he wasn't going to risk his own skin for anybody else. Some men were like that. Fargo accepted that.

But it didn't mean he had to like or respect them.

He shoved Porter out of his thoughts. The gambler wasn't worth worrying about, and there were other, more pressing matters. He told Terence, "Go over by one of the windows and listen close. If you hear anybody sneaking around out there, let me know."

The youngster nodded. "All right, Mr. Fargo." He looked a little scared, but he hadn't let that stop him from going out on the porch to join in the battle.

Fargo went over to the table and said to Maguire, "Let me have a look at that arm."

"It hurts like Hades," Maguire said as Fargo ripped his shirt sleeve to get a better look at the wound. "I can still move my arm, though. That's a good thing, ain't it?"

"Means the arrow missed the bone," Fargo agreed. "We can't pull it back out, though. The barbs on the head would do too much damage to your muscles. You might not ever be able to use the arm right again. We'll have to push it on through."

"Won't that hurt?" Ava asked.

Fargo nodded. "Yes, but it'll be better in the long run."

Maguire nodded weakly. "I know what you're talkin' about, Fargo. Go ahead and do what has to be done."

"Do you have any whiskey here?"

Either Matthew or Patrick said, "We know where Pa hides his bottle!"

"Want us to get it for you?" the other twin asked.

"You boys hush and don't bother Mr. Fargo," Ava admonished them. She walked over to a trunk that sat in a corner of the room, opened it, and took a bottle from under some clothing. She brought it back to Fargo, who took it and pulled the cork with his teeth.

"Take a slug of this and then give it back to me," he told Maguire as he handed the bottle to him. "Not too much, though. The bottle's only about half full."

Maguire nodded and lifted the bottle with his good hand. He took a drink. "I'll be all right now," he said as he gave the whiskey back to Fargo.

"Take your belt off and put it between your teeth, unless you've got something else to bite on."

Colleen asked, "What about the piece of leather we use to pick up the coffeepot?"

Fargo nodded. "Perfect."

When Maguire had his teeth tightly clamped on the thick piece of leather, Fargo took hold of the stationkeeper's arm with his left hand. Then he grasped the shaft of the arrow with his right.

"I'll count to three," he said, and then before counting at all he shoved the arrow hard, pushing the head on through Maguire's arm. Blood gushed as the head tore its way free. Maguire groaned in agony and bit down hard on the leather.

"Oh, my God!" Ava cried. "He's bleeding so bad!"

Fargo knew the wound looked worse than it really was. Moving quickly, he drew the Arkansas toothpick and cut the arrowhead off the shaft. Then he pulled the shaft out of Maguire's arm. Maguire's head slumped down on the table. He was half-senseless from the pain.

Picking up the whiskey bottle again, Fargo drenched both entrance and exit wounds, letting the fiery stuff flow deeply into the channel that the arrow had cut into Maguire's arm. Then he said to Ava, "Use clean cloth and wrap it up as tight as you can. That ought to stop the bleeding. His arm will be mighty stiff and sore for a while, but it should heal up just fine."

Ava was as pale as her husband, but she nodded and set to work, evidently grateful to have something to do that would help.

Wearily, Fargo scrubbed a hand across his face and went over to where Terence stood by one of the windows. "Hear anything out there?" he asked the youngster.

Terence shook his head and then swallowed hard. "Nothing except a . . . a sort of moaning. It went on for a while and then stopped."

Fargo nodded. He knew what Terence had heard—one of the wounded Indians had moaned in pain for a short time and then died. From the horrified look on Terence's face, he had figured it out, too.

"What do we do now, Mr. Fargo?" Terence went on.

"Wait for morning," Fargo said, quietly enough so that the others couldn't hear, "and hope they don't decide to try to burn us out before then."

Terence's eyes widened. "Could they do that?"

"They might," Fargo said. "If they do, we'll have to fight again. We won't have any choice."

"Why are you telling me this?"

Fargo put a hand on the youngster's shoulder. "Because, right now, you're the man of this family, Terence. Your pa's hurt, and he won't be much good for a while. So it's going to be up to you and me to take care of things. Can you handle it?"

Terence looked scared, and for a second he was a little boy again. But then his shoulders squared and a look of resolution came into his eyes. His voice was firm as he said, "I can handle it, Mr. Fargo."

Fargo smiled. "I never doubted it, son."

3

The night was a long one, but it passed without any further incident. Behind the thick walls of the relay station, Fargo figured they were safe from just about anything except fire. He stayed awake all night, sniffing the air often to check for even a hint of smoke.

He knew they had killed at least four or five of the Indians, and those losses might have been high enough for the Paiutes to decide to leave the station alone. On the other hand, the deaths of their fellow warriors might enrage the surviving members of the war party and make them more determined than ever to kill the whites.

In the back of the room were partitioned-off sleeping quarters for the Maguire family. Ava helped her husband to bed, where Maguire would try to sleep off some of the effects of his wound, such as losing so much blood. The twins turned in, too, but everyone else stayed up, too tense to do more than doze occasionally in a chair. Along toward dawn, Fargo caught a few winks in one of the rockers, but only after Terence assured him that he was awake and would stay that way.

When the light of day showed in the cracks around the shutters and the door, Fargo lifted the bar aside, picked up his Henry, and got ready to go outside.

"You want me to go with you, Mr. Fargo?" Terence asked.

Fargo shook his head. "No, you stay in here and keep your rifle handy, just in case you need to cover me. I'm going to take a quick look around and check on the animals in the barn."

He had started worrying about the Ovaro. He knew the big stallion wouldn't have let the Paiutes steal him; with his flashing hooves, they would never get close enough to do that. But they could have killed the Ovaro and the other horses with arrows.

Fargo used a foot to push the door open. He had both hands on the Henry, holding it ready for instant use. As soon as the door swung back, the dogs dashed outside. They didn't bark, and when Fargo risked a look, he saw that they were wandering around the area between the house and the barn, sniffing at things and peeing on them as if without a care in the world.

Fargo stepped outside and saw right away that the bodies of the Paiutes who had been killed in the fight the night before were gone. Their comrades had slipped in while it was dark and carried the bodies away. That came as no surprise to Fargo. He knew that each tribe had its own death and burial rituals, and it was very important to them that those rites be followed.

The Indians hadn't been able to get rid of the bloodstains on the porch and on the ground, though. Those grim splotches were mute evidence of what had happened here.

Fargo walked across to the barn. He used the barrel of the Henry to push back one of the double doors. No one was lurking inside. He looked into the stall where he had left the Ovaro the previous evening and saw that the black-and-white stallion was fine. The Ovaro tossed his head in greeting.

"I'm glad to see you, too, big fella," Fargo said with a smile.

The other horses and the handful of cows were also all right. Considering the circumstances, the Maguire family had gotten off astonishingly light, with Sam's wounded arm being the only real damage to them or their home. Fargo was realistic enough to know that if he hadn't been here, things might not have worked out so well for the Maguires.

Which meant that he hated to leave. With Terence as the only able-bodied male, the family might not be able to defend itself if the Paiutes returned, intent on vengeance.

Fargo didn't fully trust Porter, either. He still wasn't sure what the gambler was doing here. He was under the impression that Porter had simply ridden in the previous day, and the Maguires had offered him their hospitality, as they would have to any traveler. But did he plan to move on, or was he going to stay here for a while?

Pausing outside the barn, Fargo looked up the slope toward the juniper-dotted mountains. The Paiutes were up there; he could feel it in his bones. He wouldn't have been surprised to discover that they were watching the station right now.

Just in case they were, he strolled nonchalantly back toward the house, letting them see that he wasn't worried about them.

"Is everything all right in the barn?" Terence asked as soon as Fargo was back in the house.

He nodded. "Yes, they didn't bother the animals. I reckon they figured it would be too petty to do something like that."

"Because what they really want is to kill *us*," Terence said.

Fargo shrugged. "Hard to know what an Indian is thinking. They might come back, or they might not."

"What happened to the bodies of the ones we killed? I noticed that they're gone."

"They came in the night and took the bodies away, so that they can be laid to rest in the proper Paiute way."

Terence frowned. "But how could they have done that? I didn't hear a thing outside all night."

"They didn't make any noise," Fargo said.

Colleen had been listening to the conversation. A shudder ran through her at Fargo's words. "To think that they were that close again," she said.

"By that time they weren't interested in anything except recovering the ones who had been killed," Fargo said.

He looked around the room. Ava Maguire was at the stove, and the smells of coffee boiling and bacon frying filled the air. The twins were sitting in front of the fireplace, playing with some figurines carved out of wood. Porter sat at the table, playing solitaire again, and Terence and Colleen were with Fargo near the door. The only one who wasn't in the room was Sam Maguire. The stationkeeper was still in bed.

Fargo cleared his throat and said, "Everyone listen for a minute." When he had their attention, he went on, "I noticed that there's a wagon in the barn. We can hitch a team of horses to it, load Sam in the back, and head for the next relay station. It might be safer there."

"You mean abandon this place?" Ava asked, staring at him. "We can't do that. This is our home."

"Besides," Terence put in, "there'll be an east-bound Pony rider coming through in a couple of days. He'll be expecting us to be here with a change of horses for him. He'll be counting on us."

"Pa would never agree to leave," Colleen added.

That was pretty much the reaction Fargo had expected from them. And to be honest, he wasn't sure they would be any safer making a run for the next relay station than they would be staying right here, forted up inside the sturdy building. But he had felt like he had to put the suggestion to them and let them make up their own minds.

"All right, then," he said. "We'll wait it out for a few days and see what happens."

"You're not going to carry that mail pouch on to the next station?" Terence asked.

"I don't think it would be a good idea to leave you folks here alone."

Terence frowned. "I could still go." He held up a hand to forestall his mother's inevitable protest. "But I don't guess that would be a good idea, either. The mail will just have to wait."

"That's right," Ava said from where she stood by the stove. "It'll still get through . . . just a little slower than usual."

With that settled, Fargo moved on to the next order of business. "We still need to get Billy Conners buried this morning. Terence, why don't you come with me to stand guard, and I'll get started on digging the grave."

"All right," Terence said with a nod. "But I'd like to dig some, too. Billy and I were friends. I sort of feel like I owe it to him."

"All right, we'll trade out on the job. Bring your rifle."

"Wait just a minute," Ava said. "Breakfast is almost ready. You can at least sit down and eat a little before you . . . you start digging a grave."

Fargo thought about it for a second and then nodded. "All right." He didn't suppose the dead man was in any big hurry.

Sam Maguire insisted on getting out of bed and joining the others at the table for breakfast. He was still pale, and his arm was too stiff and sore for him to move it, but Fargo thought he didn't look too bad.

"I heard you talkin' about buryin' Billy," Maguire said as they ate. "I wish I could help with the grave—"

"Don't worry about that, Pa," Terence said. "Mr. Fargo and I will take care of it."

"But I'll read from the Book over him when you're done," Maguire went on. "Billy was a fine lad. He deserves to have some words said over him."

Fargo nodded and said, "I didn't really know him, but I expect he'd be pleased by that."

"Funerals are for the living, not the dead," Porter drawled, speaking up for the first time this morning. "Once you're gone, nothing matters to you."

"Why . . . why, that's almost blasphemous, Mr. Porter!" Ava said. "You make it sound like there's no life after death, no heavenly reward for enduring all the toil and travail in this life."

"That's exactly what I mean, madam. Man's destiny is to be nothing more than food for the worms."

Ava glared at him. "Please, sir! I'll thank you not to talk like that in front of the little ones."

The twins looked at each other, and one said, "Does he mean worms are gonna eat us?"

The other twin started to sniffle. "I don't wanna be et by worms!"

Ava tried to calm them, all the while shooting daggers with her eyes at Porter, who shrugged and said, "My apologies, Mrs. Maguire. I didn't mean to disturb anyone."

"Maybe you should help us dig that grave, Porter," Fargo said in a flinty voice.

"I'm afraid I'm not much good at physical labor."

"You can watch for Indians," Fargo snapped. "I know I can trust you to keep a good eye out, since your hide will be on the line, too."

"Whatever you say, Fargo. I'm not much of one for arguing, either."

Anger glittered in Porter's eyes as he spoke, though. Fargo knew that he had made an enemy of the gambler. Given their personalities, it had been as natural and inevitable as the sun coming up that morning.

When breakfast was over, Fargo, Terence, and Porter went outside, Fargo and Terence carrying their rifles with them. Evidently Porter didn't have any weapons except the pistol he had placed on the table the night before during the Indian attack. Terence fetched a shovel from the barn, and then they looked for a good place to bury Billy Conners.

"We haven't had to bury anybody so far," Terence explained. "Nobody's died since we've been here."

"Was the station built for the Pony Express?" Fargo asked as the three of them walked around behind the barn.

"No, it used to be a station on the stage line that went through here. That line closed down, and Russell, Majors, and Waddell bought the stations to use for the Pony Express."

"What did your father do before he went to work for them?"

"Pa's run stage stations all over the place . . . Colorado, New Mexico, Arizona, Texas . . . He was even superintendent of part of the old Butterfield Line for a while. We've moved around all my life and lived in a bunch of different places. But he says this Pony Express is the comin' thing and figures we'll be here runnin' this station from now on. Says there might even be a town grow up around it someday."

That was a nice dream, but Fargo doubted if it would ever come true. In the few months of its operation so far, the Pony Express had really caught the public's fancy. There had been many stories about it in the newspapers and illustrated magazines back east.

But Fargo knew that Western Union was already working on stringing telegraph lines that would eventually link both sides of the continent, probably within the next year or two. He had even guided some of the surveyors for the company and helped to protect some of their work parties. It was only a matter of time before people would be able to send messages instantly from one side of the country to the other, just by tapping a telegraph key.

And when that day came, there would no longer be any need for the Pony Express.

He didn't say any of that to Terence Maguire. There was no point in telling the boy that his father's dreams probably wouldn't come true. Instead he pointed to a fairly level stretch of grassy ground and said, "Maybe that would be a good spot for the grave."

"Yeah," Terence agreed. "The ground'll be a little hard, but that's true everywhere around here. We like to never got the well dug."

"We'd better get started, then." Fargo turned and held out the Henry to Porter. "I reckon you know how to use a rifle?"

"Of course," the gambler said. He took the Henry. "With two of us standing guard while one man digs, we should be able to spot any sign of trouble before it gets here."

"Let's hope so," Fargo said. He grunted as he drove the blade of the shovel into the stubborn ground.

Maguire and Terence had both been right about it being hard digging. Sweat popped out on Fargo's brow after a while. Terence took the shovel and dug for a spell, but Porter pointedly ignored the hard stare Fargo sent in his direction.

From time to time Fargo glanced up at the peaks. He still felt the eyes of the Paiutes on him. They would be watching, and they would know what the hole in the ground was for. What they couldn't know was *who* it was for. Fargo supposed they were happy about it anyway. Any dead white man pleased them, just as some whites felt that the only good Indian was a dead Indian.

Finally the grave was deep enough and long enough. Fargo tossed the shovel aside and said, "I'll get Billy out of the barn."

"I'll fetch the folks," Terence said.

Billy Conners' body seemed even lighter than it had the day before. Fargo carried the canvas-shrouded shape out of the barn and around to the grave site. "Give me a hand," he said to Porter, and his tone was so sharp the gambler didn't argue. He took one end of the bundle and helped Fargo lower it into the hole.

The Maguire family trooped out of the house and walked toward the barn with Sam Maguire in the lead. He wore his wounded arm in a black sling now and had a Bible in the other hand. Everyone gathered around the grave, with Fargo standing at one end and Porter at the other.

With his wife Ava close beside him, Maguire opened the Good Book and read the Twenty-third Psalm. When he came to the concluding line and intoned, " 'And I will dwell in the house of the Lord forever,' " the other members of the family all murmured, "Amen."

Maguire closed the black, leather-bound volume. "Billy Conners was a fine young man and a diligent Pony Express rider. Nothing ever slowed him except death, and he did his best to outrun that, accordin' to Mr. Fargo. Lord, if You have fast horses in Heaven and ever need a message delivered, I hope You'll give it to Billy. He'll get it through for You, You can count on that. We ask that You welcome him into Your house, and have mercy on his soul so that his rest will be a peaceful one. Amen."

Again the others murmured, "Amen," including

Fargo this time. Porter stood at the other end of the grave, stone-faced.

"I reckon that's all," Maguire said after a moment of silence. He was about to turn away when Terence touched his arm.

"Pa, look up there," the youngster said, a mixture of fear and excitement putting an edge in his voice.

Maguire lifted his head to look at the mountains. Puffs of white smoke rose into the clear blue sky.

"Smoke signals!" Maguire exclaimed. "But who are them red devils talkin' to?"

Fargo already knew the answer to that. He said, "Look to the west, out across the desert."

Maguire and everyone else turned to look where Fargo indicated. They saw the ominous puffs of white smoke rising out there, too.

"Blast it!" Maguire said. "They're on both sides of us now!"

Fargo nodded. "The bunch that attacked here last night is calling for reinforcements. Looks like they're going to get them, too."

"Maybe we should try for that other station after all," Porter suggested.

Maguire shook his head. "Wouldn't do any good. That smoke is between here and there. They've got us boxed in, good an' proper."

"Does that mean they'll attack the station again?" Ava asked nervously.

"They'll attack," Fargo said with certainty, "but not until they're good and ready."

"When will that be?" Terence asked.

"No way of knowing. Could be tonight, could be a few days from now. But sooner or later, they'll be coming."

"We'll just have to be ready for 'em," Maguire said. "We've got plenty o' food and ammunition, and we'll refill our water barrels while we've got the chance."

"Better wet down your roof as best you can, too," Fargo suggested. "Just because they didn't use fire arrows last night doesn't mean they won't try it next time."

Maguire nodded. "We got to get busy," he said.

"Terence and I will fill in this grave, then we'll see about fortifying the house even more."

Maguire shepherded the rest of his family back to the house while Fargo and Terence took turns scooping dirt back into the grave. Porter continued to stand watch. The gambler eyed the smoke signals to east and west and said, "What do you think the chances of one man getting through would be, Fargo?"

That would depend on the man, Fargo thought. An experienced frontiersman such as himself might, just might, be able to slip past the Indians.

"I don't think you'd stand a chance, Porter," he said bluntly. "The Paiutes will be keeping an eye on this place until they're ready to attack again. They'd see you ride away. You wouldn't get a mile before you'd have company."

"Maybe I could outrun them . . . on one of those fast Pony Express horses."

Fargo had already figured out which of the horses in the barn belonged to Porter. It was a chestnut gelding that wasn't a bad mount, necessarily, but wasn't in the same league as the swift Pony Express horses.

"You'd have to talk to Maguire about that . . . but if I was you, I'd stay right here and try to wait out this trouble."

"Could be you just want an extra gun to help defend the place," Porter said coolly.

"I'd be lying if I said that wasn't a good thing. Everybody's chances will be better if we stick together."

Porter sighed. "It looks like I don't have much choice." He chuckled humorlessly. "We all hang together or we hang separately, as the old saying goes."

"That's right," Fargo said, "except the Paiutes won't hang us. . . . They're not that merciful."

The day passed a lot more quickly than the preceding night had, because everyone was busy, even Sam Maguire, who insisted that his wounded arm wasn't enough to make him stand by and do nothing while everybody else was getting ready to fight the Indians.

Ava and Colleen brought vegetables up from the root cellar. The twins proved surprisingly adept at milking the cows. Terence carried buckets of water up a ladder to the roof of the house and wet it down as best he could, then moved over to the barn and repeated the process there.

Fargo studied the barn, especially the door into the hayloft. It faced the house, and late that afternoon he pointed it out to Maguire and said, "I think we ought to put somebody up there with a rifle. That way if the Paiutes try to get into the front of the house, we'll have them in a cross fire."

"That sounds like a fine idea," Maguire agreed, "and I'd say that you're the man for the job, Fargo. You're damn sure the best shot of any of us."

Fargo nodded slowly. "That's what I was thinking, too, but I'm glad you agree with me, Sam."

"We're going to load every gun in the house and have them ready. I can handle a pistol, even with this bad arm, so I'll take one of the windows and Terence will man the other. Ava and Colleen can load for us."

"Is there a back door?" Fargo hadn't seen one, but he wasn't sure.

Maguire shook his head. "No, but there's a window. We can give Porter the job o' seein' that none o' the savages get in there. That is . . . if you think we can trust him."

Fargo and Maguire were standing outside, near the barn, and the gambler was in the house, Fargo supposed. He said, "To be honest, I *don't* trust him much, but he's the sort of man who will do whatever is necessary to protect his own skin. You can tell him to watch that rear window and be reasonably sure that he'll do it."

"That's pretty much my thinkin', too. He wasn't expectin' to do more than spend the night here when he stopped in yesterday, but he wasn't countin' on bein' boxed in by Injuns, neither."

By evening, all the tasks had been assigned and all the preparations had been made, at least the ones that reasonably could be. It would have been nice to have a troop of cavalry on hand, Fargo reflected with a grim smile, but they weren't very likely to get that.

As darkness fell, he took some biscuits and salted beef that Ava had prepared for him and crossed over to the barn, slipping inside and pulling the door closed behind him. The Ovaro nickered softly as he caught Fargo's scent.

"I'll be counting on you to let me know if anybody comes skulking around here, big fella," Fargo told the stallion. With his Henry rifle, a couple of boxes of ammunition, and the cloth-wrapped bundle of food, he climbed the ladder to the hayloft and settled himself next to the door, which was pulled most of the way shut. He left it that way, with a narrow opening so that he could keep an eye on the front of the house, and slowly ate the food he had brought with him.

Fargo hoped that by waiting until after dark to come over here, the Paiutes wouldn't know that he was inside the barn. That way the element of surprise would be on his side if it came down to a fight. Of course, they might not even attack tonight.

Fargo recalled the name of the war chief Maguire had mentioned—Satonga. What the Paiutes did would depend on just how cunning, and how patient, this Satonga was. Fargo wouldn't put it past him to wait,

41

to draw out the suspense and the worry until it became almost agonizing for the potential victims. That sort of mental torment was well known to anyone who had done much Indian fighting.

The faint creak of one of the big doors opening below made him tense and grip the Henry tighter. A Paiute warrior could be sneaking in here to set the barn on fire or accomplish some other mischief. Or it could be one of the members of the Maguire family, although Fargo had told them all to stay inside the house until the next morning. It could even be William Henry Porter, out to steal one of the Pony Express horses and make a run for it anyway, despite what Fargo had told him. Fargo edged toward the ladder as stealthy footsteps crossed the barn floor below.

He heard the rungs of the ladder creak next. Whoever had crept into the barn was climbing up to the hayloft. That let Porter out; the gambler had no reason to come up here. He didn't think one of the Paiutes would, either. That left the Maguires.

Fargo waited. His eyes had adjusted to the darkness inside the barn, which was relieved only by faint starlight that worked its way in through holes and cracks. Fargo's eyes were keen enough, though, that he could make out the figure that reached the top of the ladder, even in these thick shadows. The shape was too big to be one of the twins, and Fargo caught a hint of a fragrance that told him it didn't belong to Terence.

It was woman-smell, the indefinable something that came from soap and clean hair and soft skin. Since Fargo didn't think that Ava Maguire would be coming up here to visit him, that left only one possibility.

"Hello, Colleen," he said.

4

She gasped in surprise, exclaiming, "Oh, my God!" and taking a sudden step backward. Then she wailed, "Oh! Oh, no!" and began to windmill her arms as she fought to keep her balance at the edge of the hayloft.

Fargo stepped forward quickly, grabbed one of her arms, and pulled her away from the brink, toward him. She was still off-balance and out of control, so she crashed into him and knocked him backward. Fargo lost his feet and went down, and Colleen came with him. Both of them sprawled out, their fall cushioned by the hay all around them.

Well aware that he had his arms full of soft, warm, sensuously curved woman, Fargo forced a stern edge into his voice as he said, "Colleen, what are you doing out here? I told you and the rest of your family to stay inside the house."

He noticed that she didn't seem to be in any hurry to get off of him. She moved a little, but her body remained in firm contact with his. In fact, her pelvis seemed to be pressing a little harder against his groin than it had been just a moment earlier.

"I didn't think you should be out here by yourself, Mr. Fargo," she said. "If the Paiutes attack, you might need somebody to . . . to load your guns for you."

"You're supposed to be doing that for your father and brother inside the house," Fargo pointed out.

Colleen shook her head. Fargo knew that because her long red hair brushed against his face. He felt her warm breath against his cheek as she replied, "My mother and the twins can handle that chore just fine. Matthew and Patrick are real go-getters."

"Well, I don't need any help—"

"I can shoot, too," Colleen broke in. "Just ask my father. He'll tell you I'm a good shot."

Dryly, Fargo said, "I don't think I'll be asking your father to confirm anything you told me while we're lying together in a hayloft. He could be a mite touchy about that."

"Oh, don't worry about *that*," Colleen said easily. "It's not like I'm a virgin or anything."

Fargo's eyebrows went up, even though he knew she couldn't see his reaction in the thick darkness inside the barn.

"I was married and everything," Colleen went on. "So I know all about what men and women do together, Mr. Fargo . . . Skye. Is it all right for me to call you Skye?"

Considering the way she was wiggling against him, and no doubt feeling the hardness at his groin that her actions had aroused, that little bit of familiarity didn't seem uncalled for. Fargo said, "That's fine. But . . . what happened to your husband?"

Colleen grew still. "He died," she said after a moment, in a hushed voice. "About a year ago, before we came out here so Pa could work for Russell, Majors, and Waddell. He was running a stagecoach station down in Texas at the time, and Dave—my husband, Dave Ashe—was one of the drivers. My name is really Colleen Ashe."

Fargo realized now that he had just assumed she had never been married, that she was still Colleen

44

Maguire and probably still innocent. Given her age, it had never occurred to him to think otherwise. But if she was twenty, which she might easily be, it was certainly possible for her to have been married, and even for her to have been a widow for a year.

"He was killed in . . . in a holdup," she went on. "Outlaws shot him off the box while he was driving. I . . . I think that's one reason Pa took the job out here in Utah Territory. He wanted to get me away from the place where there were so many memories of Dave."

"I'm sorry for your loss," Fargo said, and meant it. "But you still don't need to be out here. I can handle fighting the Paiutes just fine—"

"No, Skye, you don't understand. You see . . ." She took a deep breath, which flattened her full breasts against his chest even more. "I know what it's like to . . . to lie with a man . . . and I miss it. It's been . . . a long time. And when I saw you, I knew I wanted to . . . be with you."

Fargo had been attracted to Colleen at first sight, too, but given the fact that the Maguire family was offering him their hospitality, he had resolved to withstand the temptation. It wouldn't have been the decent thing to do to mess around with Sam Maguire's virginal daughter.

Now that he knew the situation wasn't exactly what he had assumed it to be, he felt a little differently about it, but still . . .

"This is hardly the right time or place," Fargo said.

"There's never going to be a time or place that's perfect," Colleen argued. "But when people want something really bad, they have to seize whatever opportunities they have. Besides, Skye . . ." There was a momentary hitch in her voice, but then she went on. "We don't know what's going to happen. We don't know when the Indians are going to attack again or if we'll survive if they do. Don't send me away, Skye. Don't take what may be my last chance to . . . to experience something wonderful away from me."

That was the sort of line that a fella usually used on a gal to get her to do what he wanted, Fargo reflected. He knew, though, that despite being trained from girlhood not to show it, women often had lusty appetites, just as strong as the ones possessed by men. Sometimes, even stronger. And Colleen made a powerful argument, aided by the fact that she had straddled his hips with her legs and was moving again. Her breathing sped up as she rubbed against Fargo's erection through their clothes.

When her mouth came down on his in a hot, searching kiss, and her tongue slid boldly between his lips, he knew it was no use fighting her. A part of his mind would remain alert for trouble, but he gave the rest of himself over to the sensations she awoke in him.

He slipped a hand between them, down the neckline of her dress, so that the softness of one breast filled his palm. Finding the hard nipple, he stroked it with his forefinger. That caress made Colleen moan, but she didn't break the kiss. Fargo's other hand trailed down her back to the swelling curves of her rump. He pulled her dress up and discovered there was nothing underneath it but firm, rounded flesh. His fingers explored her, delving lower and lower.

Suddenly, Colleen jerked her head up and gasped, "Got to . . . got to get these clothes off!" She sat up, and Fargo could tell by the sound of her movements that she pulled the dress up and over her head and shoulders, then tossed it to the side in the hay. When she stretched out atop him again, she was gloriously nude.

He filled both hands with her breasts and brought his head to each of them in turn. He sucked each nipple into his mouth and laved the area around it with his tongue. They grew so hard they stuck out a good half inch. Fargo nipped lightly at each one with his teeth, and that made Colleen cry out and pump her hips as if his manhood were already buried inside her.

She wasn't ready for that just yet, though. She put her hands on his shoulders and whispered, "Kiss me, Skye. Kiss me . . . down there."

Fargo had been heading there anyway, so he was glad to oblige. He rolled Colleen onto her back and then trailed kisses over her rib cage and belly. She was breathing in short little gasps that made her stomach rise and fall rapidly. He moved his hand between her legs, stroking his fingers through the triangle of hair at the juncture of her thighs. He found her core, discovered that it was already slick and hot. He teased a fingertip along her cleft.

Kneeling between her widespread legs, Fargo used his thumbs to peel back the wings of her sex, exposing her fully to him. He lowered his head and licked from top to bottom of her opening, tasting the sweet dew that had already formed there. He lingered at the top, flicking the tip of his tongue against the sensitive nubbin of flesh that he found there. Colleen cried out again in sheer ecstasy.

Fargo continued his oral caresses until Colleen was panting and gasping and squeezing her thighs hard around his head. He speared his tongue into her and sent her over the edge into a shuddering climax. She arched her back and drove her femininity against his face. Fargo cupped her rump in his strong hands and delved as deeply inside her as he could. After long, throbbing moments, she subsided with a satisfied sigh.

They weren't finished, though. Fargo knew she was right—given the perilous nature of their circumstances, this might be the last time for both of them. So he wanted to make it as good for her as he possibly could and also get the maximum amount of pleasure

47

for himself out of the encounter. While she lay there catching her breath, he pulled off his boots and stripped off the buckskin shirt and trousers. When he was nude, he moved into her embrace again.

"Oh, Skye!" she said as she reached down to close one hand around his shaft. He was so hard and thick her fingers didn't reach all the way around him. As he poised himself between her legs, she guided the head of his member to her drenched opening. Slowly but forcefully, he entered her, penetrating her until every inch of his manhood was inside her.

Then he drew back until he was almost out of her before driving forward again with a powerful flexing of his hips. Colleen lifted her knees high and locked her ankles together over his buttocks so that he could achieve the deepest possible penetration. She wrapped her arms around his neck and pulled his mouth down to hers. He penetrated her here as well, thrusting his tongue into her mouth so that he could explore the warm, wet cavern. Her tongue circled his in a sensuous duel that made passion roar higher in both of them.

Two had genuinely become one. The rhythm with which Fargo drove in and out of her gradually grew faster and more urgent. She clutched at him with greater strength. His resolve to remain aware of his surroundings and what was going on outside the barn was almost overwhelmed by the emotions coursing through him.

Almost . . . but not quite. Even in the grip of incredible passion, a part of Fargo was still the Trailsman, still ready for trouble if it should come calling.

But he sure as hell hoped it would hold off for a while longer!

Again and again and yet again he thrust into her, and her hips bucked as she met those moves with thrusts of her own. Fargo felt his climax boiling up, and as Colleen began to spasm again underneath him, he knew there was no need to hold back. That was good, because he wasn't sure if he would have been able to. He surrendered to the culmination that exploded through him, flooding her with the juices that erupted from his member in spurt after white-hot spurt. Colleen jerked and heaved beneath him in her own climax as he filled her.

Both of them shuddered a little as they came spiraling down off the peak they had reached together. Despite the coolness of the night, a fine sheen of sweat covered their bodies. Colleen made a little noise of disappointment in her throat as Fargo's softening member slipped out of her. But she cuddled against his side as he rolled onto his back and put an arm around her. He could feel her heart racing.

"Skye, I . . . I don't know how to thank you," she whispered when she got her breath back enough to be able to talk again.

"I don't reckon you owe me any thanks," Fargo said. "It's usually the other way around when it comes to things like this."

She lifted her head a little. "With the man thanking the woman, you mean?"

"Yeah."

Colleen laughed softly. "That's because you men are too thickheaded to know just how much the women want it, too. At least, most men are that way. I'm not sure about you, Skye Fargo. I think maybe you know women a little too well."

Fargo chuckled but didn't say anything. Colleen nestled herself against him again.

"Really," she said after a moment, "if . . . if that was the last time, then I couldn't have ever asked for more, Skye. If tonight is the last night, then I . . . I'll die a happy, satisfied woman."

"Nobody's going to die," Fargo said. "Not if I can do anything about—"

He fell silent abruptly and raised his head to listen intently, and after a few seconds, Colleen asked, "What is it, Skye? What's wrong?"

"Gunshots," Fargo said as he sat up and reached for his clothes. "Gunshots and hoofbeats. Somebody's coming, Colleen, and it sounds like they're bringing trouble with them."

They dressed hurriedly, taking only a few minutes to get their clothes pulled on. Then as Fargo pushed the hayloft door out farther and knelt in the opening with the Henry in his hand, he said over his shoulder to Colleen, "Get back to the house as quick as you can. Call out to your father and brother before you go in, though. Don't want either of them to get spooked and shoot you by accident."

"I'll tell them I brought some water out here to you."

Fargo nodded. "That's fine." He didn't really care what she told her family, as long as she was back behind those thick stone-and-log walls before the approaching trouble reached the relay station.

He heard the snarling crackle of several handguns being fired and the occasional heavier report of a rifle. Blended with the shots was the rolling thunder of hoofbeats. Quite a few riders were galloping down out of Black Rock Pass toward the station.

Fargo could only guess at their identity. They had to be travelers who had been jumped by the Indians as they made their way through the pass. Now they were fighting a running battle with the Paiutes. That was the only explanation that made any sense.

No matter who those desperate pilgrims might be, chances were they would stop when they reached the station. This was the closest place they could fort up. That meant more defenders when the inevitable attack on the station took place. Fargo couldn't bring himself to be happy about the bad luck that had befallen those travelers, but at least something fortunate might come out of it.

He heard the barn door shut and then saw Colleen run across the yard between house and barn. She called out when she reached the porch, as he had told her to do, and then vanished inside as the door opened. He didn't know if her parents would believe her story about bringing water out to him, but that was the least of his worries at the moment.

The shooting was more sporadic now, but the hoof-beats were louder. The moon had just risen over the mountains, and in the stark silvery light that it cast over the rugged landscape, Fargo saw a half-dozen or more riders come into view on the trail. Dust boiled up in a cloud behind them as they fogged it toward the station. From time to time one of the men turned in his saddle and fired into the roiling dust behind them. The Paiutes had to be back there, giving chase.

That was confirmed when one of the fleeing men suddenly jerked and then sagged forward over the neck of his horse. Even at this distance, Fargo's sharp eyes could make out the feathered shaft of an arrow protruding from the man's back. He stayed on his horse for a few more lunging strides but then toppled off. The man rolled over a couple of times, snapping the shaft of the arrow, and came to a stop in a limp sprawl. Fargo was reasonably certain the man was dead.

None of the others broke stride or tried to turn back to help the fallen man. They galloped on toward the relay station, which they must have spotted by now. As the riders swept up to the barn, Sam Maguire threw open the door of the house and stepped out to wave them on. Fargo heard him bellow, "In here, men, in here!"

Some of the men veered toward the house, but several reined in sharply and dropped from their saddles in front of the barn. They jerked rifles from saddle boots and ran inside, disappearing from Fargo's angle of view.

That told him they knew something about battle tactics and were not panicking. They were thinking coolly enough to have split their force so perhaps they could catch the enemy in a cross fire. He stepped to the edge of the hayloft and called to the newcomers, "Hello down there! One man come up, the rest of you stay down there for now!"

"Who the hell are you, mister?" a harsh-voiced man wanted to know.

"A friend," Fargo replied. "The Paiutes already have some folks boxed up here at this station."

He heard the men working the levers on their rifles, and then one of them started to climb the ladder to the loft. When he got there, he rumbled, "Thanks for not shootin' us when we came in. Didn't know whether or not anybody was here." The man sounded like he was middle-aged, and he wore a broad-brimmed hat with a tall, rounded crown. That was all that Fargo could tell about him in the darkness. The risen moon and the open door made it a little lighter in the hayloft, but not much.

The man joined Fargo at the opening and said, "Name's Hammond, Nate Hammond."

"Skye Fargo."

"Pleased to meet you, I reckon, Fargo." The man didn't seem to recognize the Trailsman's name, or at least if he did, he didn't say anything about it. "What is this place?"

"Pony Express relay station," Fargo replied. "The man who runs it and his family are inside the house. The Paiutes attacked us last night, but we drove them off. We expected them back, though."

"Yeah, the whole bunch of 'em are up in arms and

talkin' war," Hammond said. "They jumped us as we were ridin' through Black Rock Pass. For a minute, I didn't know if we were gonna get out of there or not."

"Did you lose any men?"

"Not until we almost made it here," Hammond replied grimly. "Then one o' them red-skinned bastards got Jed Corson. I seen him fall with an arrow in his back. Knew there was no point in tryin' to go back for him. That would've just got more of us killed."

"Yes, I saw him get hit. You were lucky not to lose anybody before that, if the Paiutes chased you all the way down from the pass."

Hammond leaned his rifle against the wall of the barn for a moment, took off his high-crowned hat, and sleeved sweat off his forehead. "They chased us, all right," he said as he replaced the hat. "Ever' damn step of the way. I ain't likely to ever forget that race, neither, what with them whoopin' and howlin' right behind us and arrows flyin' all around our heads."

Fargo knew it must have been a harrowing few minutes. Hammond and all of his companions but one had made it through, though, and now they at least stood a chance of surviving.

"Where the hell are them Paiutes?" Hammond went on. "They was right behind us, practically on our heels."

"They know the relay station is here," Fargo said. "They must have figured that they'd be riding into a cross fire and maybe more trouble than they can handle if they came on. I'll bet they stopped to try to figure out what to do next."

"You mean we got away from 'em?"

"Oh, they're still out there." Fargo grunted as he watched the surrounding terrain carefully. "Don't make a mistake about that. We're still pinned down here. There's just more of us now."

"Yeah." Hammond rubbed his jaw, beard stubble

rasping on his fingertips. "There's six of us fellas left. How many you got?"

"Sam Maguire—he's the stationkeeper here—took an arrow in the left arm last night, but he can still handle a six-gun. And his son Terence, who's about sixteen, doesn't lose his head in a fight and can use a rifle. But that's it except for Maguire's wife and daughter and a couple of twin boys who are too young to be counted on for much."

"Nobody else?" Hammond asked, with an intensity that seemed a little odd to Fargo.

"There's one other man. I almost forgot about him. Name's Porter. I don't know much about him, but I think he's a gambler."

"Is that so? Well, he's probably a pretty good shot, too."

"I wouldn't know about that," Fargo said. "Haven't seen him shoot yet. I probably will before this is all over, though."

Hammond didn't say anything to that. He just crouched beside the open hayloft door with his rifle clutched in his hands and said hoarsely, "Damn, I almost wish those red savages would come on and get it over with! Waitin' for 'em to attack is worse'n actually fightin' 'em."

He didn't know it, but he was echoing the thoughts Fargo had had earlier. Satonga was going to bide his time.

As if to prove that theory, the minutes continued to drag slowly by. The moon rose higher, and the light from it grew brighter. Hammond craned his neck to look out the hayloft door at the silvery orb.

"Would you look at that big ol' moon?" he said. "Gonna be bright as day out there pretty soon. Down Texas way, we call that a Comanche moon—"

Something whipped past his head and struck the

hayloft door with a solid thump. Hammond yanked his head back inside hurriedly and said, "Shit!"

Fargo looked at the arrow quivering in the wood and said, "Maybe we'd better call it a Paiute moon, because here they come!"

Orange flame flared from gun muzzles here and there as the Paiutes used the rifles they had captured over time from the whites that they battled. Not many of the Indians were armed with guns, however. Most used bows and arrows. Fargo and Hammond bellied down in the loft and let the deadly missiles arch over their heads. Several arrows came through the opening, fired by wildly galloping warriors who raced their ponies through the gap between the house and the barn.

The Paiutes had approached the relay station stealthily, so that there was no warning until they were almost on top of the place. Fargo estimated that there were close to fifty men in the war party. Those reinforcements had arrived.

But the defenders had been reinforced, too. Pistols and rifles cracked wickedly as the men in the house and in the barn opened fire on the marauding Indians. Fargo and Hammond crawled forward until they had a good view of the attackers, and the men who were below in the barn made good use of the rifle slits that had been left in the walls when the barn was constructed.

The Henry cracked and jumped in Fargo's hands as he fired, levered, fired again. He was rewarded by the sight of a couple of Paiute braves flying off their ponies. The bullets from the other defenders were taking a toll, too. The attackers began to mill around, rather than charging back and forth in a cohesive unit. One of the Indians, with a large, feathered headdress, shouted something. Fargo drew a bead on the man and blasted a slug all the way through his body. The

55

Paiute threw up his hands and slid loosely off his horse.

Fargo knew better than to hope that he had just killed Satonga. The man in the headdress was probably just a subchief of some sort who had been placed in charge of this attack. Satonga himself would be up there on one of the overlooking hills, watching the battle but not taking part in it, like any good general.

Sooner or later, though, Satonga would be drawn into the fight. Maybe not this particular ruckus, but if the defenders won again, as they appeared to be on the verge of doing, the Paiute warriors might insist that Satonga lead them personally into battle the next time. They might decide that their medicine would never be strong enough to defeat the whites without their leader taking a hand himself.

Fargo hoped it came to that. That would mean that he and the Maguires and the others had successfully defended the relay station yet again.

And it would give him a chance to put some lead into Satonga. If he could kill the war chief, there was at least a chance that the other Paiutes would give up these raids.

Gunfire continued to roll from the house and the barn. Several more raiders were hit, and then the others stopped their confused milling and galloped away from the station, heading up into the mountains again.

"Let's get out there and send 'em on their way proper-like!" Nate Hammond enthused.

"Hold on," Fargo said. "They may just be trying to draw us out so that they can double back and hit us again while some of us are out in the open."

"Yeah, I reckon," Hammond agreed, but he didn't sound happy about it. "Sure wish I could take a few more shots at them red heathens, though."

Fargo stood up and leaned out the hayloft door. The Paiutes were still moving. They had left behind half a dozen of their number, the bodies scattered around the open area between the house and the barn.

When the war party was completely out of sight, Fargo said, "All right, let's go down there and check on those wounded men."

"I want to see if any o' my pards are hurt, too," Hammond said. He went down the ladder first, followed by Fargo, who was equally anxious to find out if anyone inside the house had been wounded.

When he reached the bottom of the ladder, Fargo turned and saw Hammond standing in the open doorway of the barn with two more men. "Your friends all right?" Fargo asked.

Hammond nodded. "Yeah. We'll check on those Injuns who got left behind and make sure they're all dead."

Fargo headed for the house as Hammond and the other two men approached the fallen Paiutes, guns held at the ready in case any of the wounded men were still alive and eager to fight. By the time Fargo reached the house, the front door was opening. Sam Maguire emerged first, followed closely by Terence and Colleen.

"Skye, are you all right?" Colleen asked worriedly as she hurried past her father and brother.

"I'm fine," he told her. "A few of those arrows came close, but that's all. What about you?"

"No one was hurt inside, thank goodness."

From the porch, Maguire said, "We sent 'em packin' again, Fargo. Think they'll give up this time and leave us alone from now on?"

"Hard to say," Fargo replied, "but I doubt it. We've hurt them enough now so that Satonga will feel like he has to kill us to save face with the rest of the tribe."

Maguire nodded slowly. "I was afraid you'd say that. I was thinkin' the same thing."

Before they could say anything else, one of Hammond's friends suddenly called out, "Hey, this one's alive!"

Fargo swung around and saw that the man was standing over one of the fallen Paiutes, his rifle trained on the wounded warrior. Hammond strode quickly toward them, asking, "How bad is he hurt?"

"Not too bad," the other man replied. "Looks like a bullet creased his skull and knocked him out. He's startin' to come to."

Fargo walked toward them, thinking that perhaps if the injured Paiute spoke any English, he could be questioned about Satonga's plans. The chances of getting any useful information out of him were slim, but Fargo was willing to try to interrogate him, at least.

But Hammond got there first, and as he reached the wounded man's side, he leaned down and tangled his left hand in the Paiute's long black hair. He jerked the warrior's head up.

"What are you—" Fargo began.

Before he could finish the question, Hammond drew a knife with a long, heavy blade from a sheath at his hip and swiped the blade across the wounded Paiute's tight-drawn throat. Blood fountained from the gaping wound left behind by the knife, splattering blackly across the dirt in the silvery moonlight. The Paiute jerked spasmodically and then died.

5

Fargo was so shocked by the wanton cruelty of what he had just witnessed that for a few seconds all he could do was stare. During that short interval, Hammond let go of the Indian's hair and stepped back. The Paiute's head fell forward and smacked face-first into the ground.

"There," Hammond said in satisfaction. "That'll take care o' him." He looked around. "Any of the others still alive?"

"No, I reckon he was the only one," said the third stranger, who had come over to join Hammond and the other man. "Sorry, Nate."

"I *do* like killin' me a filthy redskin whenever I get the chance," Hammond said. "It's even better when it's close up like that, so you can see the bastard's eyes and know that he knows he's about to die."

The callousness of the man's tone jolted angry words out of Fargo's mouth. "What the hell did you do that for?" he demanded.

Hammond looked at him with what appeared to be genuine surprise. "Do what? Cut that Injun's throat?"

"That's right."

Hammond shrugged. "To kill him, of course. Quickest and easiest way to do it. Could've shot him in the head, I reckon, but that would've wasted a bullet."

He chuckled. "Besides, they kick better when their throat's cut."

On the porch of the house, Sam Maguire put a hand on his daughter's arm and said, "Get back in the house, Colleen. You go with her, Terence." Both of the young people looked horrified by what they had just seen.

Fargo was horrified, sickened, and angered. "You had no call to do that, Hammond," he snapped.

"Why the hell not?" Hammond said, his forehead corrugating in a frown. "You think that buck wouldn't'a cut *your* throat if he'd got the chance, Fargo?"

"That's not the point—"

"Then what is the point?" Hammond broke in. He waved a hand at the other bodies. "What about them other redskins who're already dead? I don't see you sheddin' no tears for them!"

"That's different," Fargo insisted.

"I don't see how."

"For one thing, they were trying to kill us when they were shot. That man wasn't a threat anymore. If we had disarmed him and tied him up, he couldn't have hurt anybody."

Hammond snorted contemptuously. "Any Injun is dangerous if he's still drawin' breath, Fargo. I'd've thought that the high-an'-mighty Trailsman would know that."

So Hammond *did* know who he was. That didn't change anything, though. Fargo said, "Whether you thought he was dangerous or not, I was planning on asking him some questions about Satonga's plans."

"You'd be wastin' your time," Hammond said with a shake of his head. "He'd likely not understand what you were sayin', and even if he did, he'd sooner spit in your face than tell you anything he thought might help you. You ought to know that, too, Fargo."

In truth, Fargo did know how unlikely it was that he could have gotten anything useful out of the wounded Paiute. But now there was no chance at all, thanks to Hammond's brutality.

But he could dwell on this, Fargo told himself, or he could let it pass and keep a more watchful eye on Hammond in the future, meanwhile being grateful that he and the Maguires had six more men on hand to help them defend the relay station. He was just enough of a pragmatist to know that he had to choose that second course of action.

"All right," he said. "Let's get these bodies dragged over there by the barn, so they won't be just lying out in the open."

Hammond and his friends grumbled a little about that, but they pitched in and helped with the grisly task. When the corpses were stacked beside the barn, Fargo went on, "We'd better post some sentries, just in case the Paiutes try anything else tonight."

"What I'd like to know is who put you in charge, mister?" Hammond asked. "Could be somebody else around here is used to givin' orders."

"I'm not giving orders. I'm just saying what's common sense. There's no telling what the Paiutes will do, so we'd be fools to let down our guard."

"He's right about that, Nate," one of the other men said.

"Yeah, yeah," Hammond said in a surly voice. "I reckon so. Dewey, you and Bagwell get in the barn and keep your eyes open. Holler or let off a shot or something if you see any savages skulkin' around."

"Sure, Nate."

Fargo and Hammond walked toward the house, the atmosphere around the two men tense and unfriendly. They had gone from being allies in the fight against the Paiutes to being . . . Fargo wasn't sure where they stood now. He knew, though, that he could never be friends with anyone who could cut another man's throat so cold-bloodedly.

As soon as they walked in the house, Colleen started toward Fargo, as if she intended to throw her arms around him. She stopped herself after only a couple of steps, though, and Fargo couldn't tell if anyone else in the room had noticed her reaction or not.

The twins were excited by everything that had been going on, and talked to each other in loud voices about all the shooting and fighting. One of them tugged on Ava's skirt as she stood by the stove heating coffee and food. "Ma!" the little boy said insistently. "Can Pat and me go out and look at the dead Injuns?"

"Heavens, no!" Ava replied.

"Aw, Ma," the other twin complained. "We never got to see a dead Injun close up before."

Maguire lumbered toward them and said, "Go on with you, you bloodthirsty little scoundrels. You should be thankin' your lucky stars you didn't see a live Injun close up!"

"And they're Indians, not Injuns," Ava added. "You'll never learn to speak properly if you don't work at it, boys."

"Don't want to speak properly," one of the twins muttered.

"Just want to look at them dead Injuns," the other one added.

Hammond went over to Maguire and extended his right hand. "You the fella who's in charge o' things around here?" he asked. "My name's Hammond, Nate Hammond."

Maguire hesitated for a second, as if unsure whether or not he wanted to shake the hand that had held the knife that cut the wounded Paiute's throat. But then his hospitable nature won out and he took Hammond's hand.

"Sam Maguire. We were mighty glad to see you and

your friends ride in, Mr. Hammond. Those Paiutes had us outnumbered by a whole heap."

"I reckon they still do," Hammond pointed out. "But when the odds are against you, anything you can do to whittle 'em down is a good thing, I always say."

"Amen to that."

Now that they were inside, in the light, Fargo was able to get a better look at Nate Hammond. The man was in his forties, as Fargo had figured, and had rugged features that had seen plenty of wind and weather. He was tall, rawboned, and muscular in a sheepskin jacket, wool shirt, and denim trousers tucked into high-topped black boots. The high-crowned, broad-brimmed hat on his straw-colored hair was black, too. His voice had a Texas twang to it.

And something about the man looked familiar to Fargo. He couldn't put his finger on what it was, but the dislike he had felt for Hammond ever since the cold-blooded killing of the wounded Paiute deepened into a definite unease. Something was wrong here, Fargo told himself.

He began to get an inkling of what it was when he realized that he hadn't seen Porter since coming into the house. Not only was there no sign of the gambler, but the three men from Hammond's group who had taken refuge in the house weren't in evidence, either. He turned to Maguire and asked, "Where's Porter?"

The stationkeeper looked around, frowning in puzzlement. "Why, he's here, ain't he?"

Fargo shook his head. "I don't see him."

"Maybe he's still back there guardin' that rear window." Maguire went over to a blanket that formed a door over a narrow hallway leading through the sleeping quarters and thrust it back. At the other end of the corridor was the narrow window that Porter had been assigned to defend.

The shutters over it stood wide open. There was no sign of the gambler.

"What in bloody blue blazes?" Maguire muttered with a frown. "Looks like he ran out on us, the damned fool. The Paiutes will get him for sure if he tries to slip past them."

Fargo felt the same way, but somehow he wasn't surprised that Porter had lit a shuck. He had seemed to want to be anywhere other than the relay station, no matter how dangerous it might be at the moment to try to flee in any direction from Black Rock Pass.

And the open window didn't solve the question of where Hammond's other companions were, either. Fargo was just about to bring that matter up, when a voice called urgently from outside.

"Nate! Nate, come out here and look what we've got!"

"Now what the devil is it?" Maguire said. He started toward the door.

"Better hold on there, friend," Hammond said as he moved to block Maguire's path. "I'll handle this."

"The hell you will!" Maguire said with an indignant snort. "This is my station. If there's anything to be handled here, I'll do it."

Hammond put his hand on the stag-butted revolver that was holstered at his hip. "Not this, Maguire. This is my business."

The situation was deteriorating rapidly, Fargo thought. Whatever was developing, he had to move to stop it now, before it got any worse. He took a step to one side and said, "Take it easy, Hammond. There's no need for trouble."

Hammond's eyes darted back and forth between Fargo and Maguire. Fargo's maneuver had flanked Hammond, so that he couldn't hope to cover both men if he drew his gun. Fargo could almost see the wheels of Hammond's brain turning as he figured the angles and the odds and then reached an unwelcome decision.

"Fine," Hammond snapped as he glared at Fargo. "I'm warnin' you, though. . . . Don't mix in with what don't concern you."

Again a call sounded from outside. "Hey, Nate!"

Hammond turned and went toward the door, but he didn't try to stop Fargo and Maguire from following him. Maguire motioned Terence back when the youngster tried to fall in with them.

"Stay in here, boy, until we find out what's goin' on," Maguire growled quietly.

Hammond stepped out onto the porch. Ugly laughter greeted him, and a man's voice added, "Looky what we got here, Nate. He ducked out the window and tried to get away after the fracas was over. Thought we hadn't spotted him yet and figured he could give us the slip again, I reckon. We went after him and brung him back, though."

"Good work, boys," Hammond said. "Didn't kill him, did you?"

"No, we figured you'd want to do that, when you were through with him. We just knocked him around a mite, to teach him he shouldn't try to run out on his old pards."

Fargo's jaw tightened as he and Maguire stood there listening to the conversation and looking at the shape huddled on the ground at the feet of Hammond's friends. Hammond's men, Fargo amended silently, since it was becoming obvious that Hammond was the one in charge of this group.

The man on the ground lifted his head, and the blood on his face showed black in the moonlight. He had been beaten, all right, and his features were somewhat swollen, but the lean face was still recognizable as that of William Henry Porter.

Hammond stalked over to Porter, and before Fargo

could even think about trying to stop him, he had drawn back his foot and kicked the gambler hard in the stomach. Porter groaned in pain and curled up into a ball.

"Howdy, Porter," Hammond said with a sneer. "Maybe next time you'll think twice before you steal from hombres who are supposed to be your partners."

Fargo stepped forward and said, "I don't know what's going on here, but that'll be just about enough of that, Hammond."

The big, rawboned man looked back over his shoulder and said, "Yeah, it'll be enough, all right . . . enough of you, Fargo." He made a sharp gesture.

Fargo started to reach for the Colt on his hip, but a metallic ratcheting that was the unmistakable sound of a gun being cocked came from behind him and made him stop the motion. Hammond's other two men had the drop on him and Maguire, and as another gun was cocked, Fargo knew that both he and the stationkeeper were covered.

"What the hell's goin' on here?" Maguire demanded furiously. "I'm in charge o' this place, Hammond—"

"You *were* in charge," Hammond cut in. "Now I'm runnin' things." He looked past Fargo and Maguire and ordered, "Take their guns."

As the hardcases behind them advanced, Fargo swiftly considered his options. When one of the gunmen came close enough to take his Colt, he could whirl around and try to knock the man's gun aside before the trigger could be pulled.

But even if he accomplished that, he realized, Hammond and the other three men were close by and clearly wouldn't hesitate to use violence to get what they wanted. They might decide to just gun down Maguire and him to simplify matters. That would leave the rest of the Maguire family at the mercy of these obviously merciless men. Fargo knew he couldn't risk that.

"Take it easy, Sam," he said quietly to Maguire. "We'll play along with them for now."

Hammond overheard the words and laughed harshly. "You'll play along from now on, Fargo," he said. "That is, unless you want a bullet in the guts."

A hand reached from behind and plucked Fargo's Colt from its holster. A moment later, the Arkansas toothpick was taken from its sheath as well. And the Henry rifle was in the house, where it wasn't going to do Fargo any good.

Maguire's revolver was confiscated, too, leaving both of them unarmed. Hammond grunted in satisfaction and turned back to Porter. He kicked the gambler again, clearly taking great enjoyment from his brutality.

"How about explaining what's going on here, Hammond?" Fargo said. "Just what is it you want?"

"What do I want?" Hammond echoed. "I want the money this bastard stole from me, and I want him to suffer for stealin' it. That's simple enough, ain't it?"

Fargo suddenly remembered where he had seen Hammond before. It had been at Bent's Fort, down in New Mexico Territory, about a year earlier. Hammond and several other men had been suspected of being part of a gang of raiders that had been attacking and looting wagon trains on the Santa Fe Trail. Before anything could be proven against them, though, they had vanished.

Now Fargo had no doubt that the charges leveled against Hammond and his men had been true. Probably since that time they had been engaged in outlawry somewhere else. And Porter had been one of them, at least for a while . . . until he had double-crossed them, stolen some of their loot, and disappeared.

Hammond wasn't the sort of man to let anybody

67

get away with that, however, so he and his companions had come after Porter, picking up his trail somewhere along the way and following him west along the Pony Express route. . . .

Until fate—and the Paiutes led by Satonga—had intervened and brought them all here to this relay station at Black Rock Pass, along with a family of innocents—and the Trailsman.

Those thoughts flashed through Fargo's mind in a matter of seconds. Confident that he had figured out the whole story, he said, "The Maguires don't have anything to do with your problem, Hammond. There's no need to hurt them."

"Hurt 'em? I don't plan to hurt nobody 'cept this double-crossin' son of a bitch Porter, unless they try to interfere with me. Soon as he tells us where he hid our money, we'll be leavin'."

That statement gave Fargo a shred of hope, but it was quickly dashed when one of the other men said, "What about the women, Nate? You said we'd take the women with us."

Hammond glared at the man briefly, as if annoyed that he had revealed too much about their plans. Beside Fargo, Sam Maguire made a low growling sound in his throat and clenched the fist on the end of his good arm.

"Yeah, might as well get it out in the open, I reckon," Hammond said. "Mrs. Maguire and her daughter are mighty fine-lookin' women, so they'll be travelin' with us for a spell after we leave here."

"You're crazy!" Maguire burst out. "If you touch one hair on their heads, I'll kill you!"

"Now there's no need to be like that," Hammond scolded. "Maybe you'd better ask that pretty little wife o' yours what *she'd* like to do. Stuck out here in the middle o' nowhere like this, she's maybe been cravin' the attention of a bunch o' handsome hombres like us—"

Hammond didn't get any farther with his coarse comments. With a roar of rage, Maguire launched himself at the outlaw, bent on shutting Hammond's filthy mouth with a fist. Before Maguire had gone more than a step, though, one of the hardcases behind him struck him in the head with a pistol, bringing the gun down in a vicious, chopping blow. Maguire stumbled and fell to his knees, stunned.

"Pa!" Terence yelled from the porch, where he had slipped out of the house to watch what was going on in defiance of his father's orders. The boy stepped to the edge of the porch and started to lift the rifle in his hands.

"Terence, no!" Fargo said as he threw himself to the side, crashing into a man who was lifting a gun to fire at the youngster. The man cursed and swung the pistol toward Fargo's head instead. Fargo ducked and hooked a hard left to the man's midsection, then followed it with a straight right that knocked him off his feet.

The sudden roar of a gun made everybody freeze.

Powder smoke curled from the barrel of the revolver in Hammond's hand as the outlaw pointed it at Terence. "Drop that rifle, boy!" Hammond commanded. "Or the next bullet'll go in you instead of up in the air."

Terence hesitated, the rifle only halfway to his shoulder. He looked at Fargo, who knew that Terence was asking him what to do.

Although the words tasted bitter in Fargo's mouth, he said, "Better do what he says, Terence. These men are dangerous . . . maybe as dangerous as those Paiutes."

Hammond chuckled. "Now you're gettin' it, Fargo.

I'd say we're *more* dangerous than a bunch o' heathen savages, 'cause we're smarter.''

Fargo wasn't sure that was true, but he didn't argue the point. Instead, he said, "Put the rifle down, Terence.''

"But . . . but they hit Pa! And they beat up Mr. Porter!''

Fargo took hold of Sam Maguire's good arm and lifted the bulky stationkeeper back to his feet. "Your pa will be all right," he told Terence. "Right now, let's just cooperate with them.''

Hammond aimed his gun carefully. "Do what Fargo says, boy, or I'm fixin' to put a bullet right between your eyes.''

With his face showing the war between fear and anger that was going on inside him, Terence slowly lowered the rifle and put it on the porch at his feet. One of Hammond's men hurried over and snatched it up.

"Now you're usin' your head," Hammond said as he lowered his gun but didn't holster it. Instead he gestured with the barrel at Porter and ordered, "Haul that bastard back inside. We'll see if he talks right away . . . or drags things out and makes 'em more entertainin'.''

Fargo and Maguire were prodded toward the house at gunpoint. Fargo could tell from the way Terence looked at him that the young man was disappointed in him. Terence thought that Fargo was giving up, that he was too scared of Hammond and the other outlaws to fight back.

That wasn't the case at all. Fargo just wanted to wait for the right moment, when he might be able to turn the tables on their captors without putting the Maguire family in too much danger. He knew he couldn't just stand by forever and hope for the best.

Because Fargo was convinced that no matter what

Hammond said, he didn't intend to leave any of them alive. Hammond had to know that Fargo and Maguire and Terence wouldn't let them ride away with Ava and Colleen without putting up a fight. So when he got good and ready, he and his men would just kill them, along with the twins.

And in the end, a similar fate probably awaited the two women. While it was possible that the outlaws might eventually let them go when they got tired of them, it was more likely they would kill them. That would make it a clean sweep, with everyone who was unlucky enough to have been caught here at the relay station wiped out.

Fargo couldn't let it get that far. But as outnumbered as he and the Maguires were, he knew he would have to outthink these killers before they would have a chance of outfighting them.

The shot Hammond had fired into the air had drawn the attention of everyone in the house, so Ava, Colleen, Matthew, and Patrick were all watching in confusion from the doorway as Fargo and Maguire were forced up onto the porch. "Get back," Hammond growled at them.

"What are you doin'?" one of the twins demanded.

"How come you're pointin' your guns at our pa?" the other one asked.

"Shut up and get inside, you little brats," Hammond snapped.

Ava faced him defiantly. "This is my house, sir," she said, "and if you're going to act like this, you're not welcome here, Indians or no Indians!"

Hammond started to respond angrily, but Fargo took advantage of the opportunity to put in, "You'd better listen to what she's saying, Hammond. Remember, those Paiutes are still out there."

Hammond frowned at him. "What do you mean by that?"

"Just that the situation really hasn't changed," Fargo said steadily. "You still need us."

"Don't know what for," Hammond said with a snort as he holstered his gun.

"What are you going to do?" Fargo asked. "Where are you going to go? You can't head back through the pass. The Paiutes have it blocked good and proper by now. You can't head west across the desert, because they're out there, too."

"You don't know that for sure."

"We saw smoke signals from that direction earlier in the day," Fargo said. "Maybe they're all gone now. If you want to risk it, that's up to you, I reckon."

"Damn right it's up to me," Hammond said, but he didn't sound quite as confident as he had a moment earlier. "What about headin' north or south?"

Fargo shook his head. "Nothing but wasteland in both directions for a hundred miles or more. Anyway, if the Paiutes see you leave here, they'll follow you and run you to ground."

"So what are you sayin'?" Hammond asked indignantly. "That we're stuck here forever?"

"Not forever. If we continue to defend the station, Satonga, the Paiute war chief, will give up sooner or later. Either that, or the army will get wind of the Paiute uprising and send in troops to put it down. The country won't stand for the Pony Express being interfered with."

Hammond's forehead creased in a worried frown. "The army?" he repeated. It was obvious he didn't want to still be around here if the army became involved.

Fargo sensed an opening. He said, "Let me talk to you alone for a minute, Hammond. We can work this out."

Hammond rasped a hand along his jaw. "Yeah, maybe . . ."

One of the other outlaws said, "Wait a minute, Nate. You're the ramrod o' this outfit, but we don't have secrets from each other, either. You can't go makin' a private deal with this hombre."

Hammond's face contorted with anger as he swung toward the man and faced him across the porch. "Like you said, Bagwell, I'm the ramrod o' this outfit! And I'll talk to whoever I want, whenever and wherever I want! If that don't sit right with you . . . you know what you can do about it."

His hand hovered over the butt of his gun.

Bagwell held up both hands, palms out. "Take it easy, Nate," he said hurriedly. "I didn't mean to put a burr under your saddle. I'm just sayin' you can't trust this fella Fargo. He might try to trick you."

"Nobody's gonna trick me," Hammond said. "Come on, Fargo. Let's take a walk out to the barn."

Now that it had become a point of honor with Hammond, Fargo knew the boss outlaw would at least listen to him. He had been careful not to reveal that he knew the truth about the gang's raids on those wagon trains down in New Mexico Territory. If Hammond suspected that Fargo knew about that, there probably wouldn't be anything Fargo could say that would convince him not to go through with his murderous plan, and likely sooner rather than later.

"Take Porter inside and tie him up," Hammond ordered his men. "Gather up all the loose guns, too. Don't want these good folks gettin' tempted to use 'em." He jerked his head at Fargo. "Come on."

They walked toward the barn. Fargo noticed that Hammond kept his hand on the butt of his gun, just in case.

When they got there, Hammond said, "What is it you want to talk to me about, Fargo?"

"Look, you're making a mistake here," Fargo said. "Whatever grudge is between you and Porter, the Maguires don't have anything to do with it, and neither do I."

"You were about to step in and defend him."

Fargo shrugged. "That was when I didn't realize what was going on. I never liked the bastard to start with. If he was dumb enough to steal from you, then it's his own lookout, and whatever happens to him is on his head."

Hammond rubbed his jaw again. "Sounds like you're gettin' smarter again."

"What you ought to do is give the Maguires their guns back, apologize to them, and tell them that all you're interested in is helping them defend this place until the Paiutes are gone. You do that, and I can guarantee that when it's all over, you can ride away with Porter and nobody will try to stop you."

"Nobody can stop me from doin' what I want to do," Hammond said. "And I don't much cotton to folks tellin' me what I ought to do, either."

"I'm just trying to help, so that nobody else gets hurt." Fargo waved a hand toward the mountains that loomed over the relay station. "There were about fifty warriors in the bunch that attacked the place earlier. But there could be a hundred more up there, or two hundred, or even five hundred. When they come back, you'll need every gun you can get, Hammond, and you'll need to be able to trust them, too. Otherwise . . ." Fargo shrugged again.

"What are you sayin'?" Hammond asked with a glare. "Are you tryin' to convince me those folks *won't* fight to save their own hides if the Indians attack again?"

"It's a matter of when, not if," Fargo said. "And why should they fight if they know that you're just going to kill them and steal the two women?"

Hammond's frown darkened. "The boys won't like it if I go back on what I promised 'em."

"Mrs. Maguire and Colleen, you mean?" Fargo shook his head. "If you get your money back from Porter, you won't have any trouble finding female companionship the next time you get to a town. Just check the nearest saloon or whorehouse."

"Out here, we're a long way from a saloon or a whorehouse," Hammond argued. "The fellas'll be mighty upset if they have to wait."

"But you're the boss," Fargo pointed out.

Hammond looked at him narrow-eyed for a moment and then said, "Don't think I'm so stupid I don't know what you're tryin' to do, Fargo . . . but that don't mean you're not right. As long as those savages are out there, all our lives are in danger. I reckon the smart thing to do would be to go along with what you said."

"Fine. You'll give the Maguires their guns back and tell them you just made a big mistake. I don't know if they'll believe you or not. It'll be up to you to convince them it's in their own best interests to cooperate with you."

"Yeah, yeah," Hammond grumbled. "I ain't used to all this negotiatin'. Most times when I want something, I just take it at the point of a gun."

"You can't take people's trust at the point of a gun. And right now, with Satonga and his warriors liable to attack again at any time, you need the Maguires to trust you and fight beside you."

"Yeah, I reckon. But there's just one thing, Fargo . . . I ain't givin' you *your* guns just yet, because *I* don't trust *you*." Hammond poked a finger against Fargo's chest. "You'll get your guns back when the arrows start to flyin' again, and not one second before!"

6

Maybe it wasn't the best deal in the world, but Fargo felt like it was the best one he could make right now. That lack of trust went both ways. He knew Hammond was lying to him, knew that in the back of his mind the outlaw still planned to kill Maguire and Terence and the twins, and kidnap Ava and Colleen. But at least the family would have their guns back, and Hammond would keep his men under control for the moment, in order not to tip his hand until after the threat of the Paiutes was over and done with.

And, of course, there was still a chance that none of them would survive the next attack, Fargo thought grimly. The whole question of who trusted who might be rendered moot by Satonga and his warriors.

With their newfound "understanding" between them, Fargo and Hammond walked from the barn back to the house. A couple of Hammond's men stood on the porch, one at each end, holding rifles and standing guard. One of them called softly, "How about it, Nate? What happens now?"

"Change o' plans," Hammond growled. "I'll fill you boys in later. For now, just keep an eye peeled for those damn redskins."

They went on into the house. Not surprisingly, the tension in the air inside the big main room was so thick Fargo could have cut it with the Arkansas toothpick—if he'd had the big knife.

The other three outlaws had spread out around the room so they could keep the Maguires covered. The members of the family all sat at the long table, huddled together on one of the benches. Maguire and Ava were side by side, his good arm draped protectively around her shoulders. The twins were beside Ava, and then Colleen and Terence, who had a fierce scowl on his face. Fargo wasn't sure who Terence was angrier at, him or the outlaws.

William Henry Porter sat in one of the rocking chairs with an arm pressed to his stomach where Hammond had kicked him. The blood on his face had dried in ugly streaks. Fargo still didn't like the gambler, but he didn't like to see any man being beaten by a gang, either.

Fargo looked at Hammond, and the outlaw glared for a second before walking over to the table. "Listen, folks," he said to the Maguires, "I made a mighty big mistake earlier. Reckon I just got carried away, what with fightin' them redskins and then findin' out that a fella I've been lookin' for was here. Porter there done me and my pards wrong, and I intend to make it right. But that's no reason to take anything out on y'all." Hammond gestured to one of his men. "Give 'em their guns back."

Maguire looked surprised, but not any more so than the three outlaws. "What?" exclaimed the man Hammond had just spoken to. "Nate, you can't mean that. What about—"

"Damn right I mean it!" Hammond said. "When them Paiutes come back, I damn sure want guns in the hands of every able-bodied man on this place."

One of the other hardcases began, "But I thought—"

"*I* do the thinkin' around here!" Hammond roared.

"Or have you boys forgotten that? I can remind you of it if I need to."

"Settle down, Nate," the outlaw called Dewey said. "If you've changed your mind, I reckon we'll go along with you."

"Damn right you will," Hammond said curtly.

The guns that had been collected earlier were stacked in one of the chairs. Dewey picked them up and carried them over to the table. Hammond reached out and took Fargo's Colt from him.

"I'll take that for now," Hammond said with a glance at Fargo, who shrugged and nodded.

Wait for it, Fargo thought. Wait for the right time. . . .

As Dewey placed the other guns on the table so that Maguire and Terence could reclaim them, one of the twins looked up at Hammond and said, "Mister, can my brother and me have guns, too?"

"What?" Hammond gave a little shake of his head, as much a gesture of surprise as it was negation. "Hell, no, you can't have guns. You're just little sprouts. Didn't your mama ever teach you nothin'?"

"Of course I did," Ava said coldly. "And for once you and I are in agreement, Mr. Hammond. I don't want them to have guns, either."

"Well . . . you're obliged . . . I reckon." Hammond sighed and shook his head again.

Dewey moved back to the position he had occupied earlier. He was the youngest of the outlaws, Fargo noted, and the only one who didn't look like he had been riding the dark trails and listening to the owl hoot for a long time. His eyes kept straying back to Colleen, too. Fargo could tell that he was attracted to her. Hammond seemed to be more interested in Ava, who was closer to his age and still a fine-looking woman despite the strands of silver in her brown hair.

Sam Maguire picked up his pistol and put it back

in its holster. He gave Hammond a hard look and said, "You said some things earlier that I ain't forgot about, mister."

"Like I told you, that was a mistake," Hammond said. "But if you think I'm gonna stand around apologizin', you're wrong."

"I don't want an apology. Just steer clear o' me and my family, elsewise there'll be a heap o' trouble. And it won't be wearin' feathers this time."

"Fine," Hammond snapped. "What about Porter?"

"Whatever business you have with him is between the two o' you. I won't have any man mistreated in my house, though."

"Fair enough." Hammond jerked a thumb toward the door. "Take him out to the barn."

As a couple of Hammond's men closed in on the gambler, Porter looked up from the chair and his eyes met Fargo's. "Aren't you going to do anything about this?" he asked.

"I don't know what you expect me to do," Fargo said. "You brought this trouble on yourself, Porter."

The gambler eyed him coldly as the pair of outlaws grabbed his arms and jerked him to his feet. "I won't forget this," he said.

Fargo made no reply. His main goal right now was to find a way for the Maguires to make it through this alive and unharmed. Porter was just going to have to take his chances.

Porter struggled in the grip of the two outlaws but wasn't able to stop them from forcing him out of the house. Hammond followed, saying over his shoulder to Dewey, "Keep an eye on things in here."

Dewey nodded. He might be the youngest member of the gang, but he also seemed to be the most levelheaded.

Fargo went over to the table and sat down on the other side from the Maguires. Sam Maguire swung around so that he could face Fargo and asked, "What happens now?"

"We wait," Fargo said. "Satonga has tried two frontal attacks on the station. He's likely to be a mite trickier the next time."

"You don't sound like you've got any doubt there'll be a next time."

"I don't," Fargo said. "No doubt at all."

As the tension in the room eased somewhat, Ava and Colleen got busy heating up food and coffee. Fargo noticed that Dewey wandered over and started trying to make small talk with Colleen, who responded mostly with monosyllables. Fargo could see Dewey's frustration growing, but the young man didn't get angry. After a while he gave a resigned little shrug and walked away.

Everyone looked up sharply as a scream of pain came from somewhere outside. Bagwell chuckled and said, "Nate's makin' sure that Porter's sorry he ever thought about crossin' us."

The fact that Porter was probably being tortured out in the barn made Fargo's jaw clench angrily. But there was another possible explanation for that scream, he realized, and he said, "One of you might want to go check on that. It could be that some of the Paiutes slipped back down here, and they've grabbed one of your friends."

Dewey, Bagwell, and the other outlaw exchanged worried glances. "You think so?" Dewey said to Fargo.

"It's possible."

Bagwell said, "Dewey, walk out to the barn and make sure Nate and the other fellas are all right."

"Me?" Dewey said. "Why not you?"

"Because I'm the one who said it first, and I'm older'n you."

"When Nate left out of here, he told *me* to keep

an eye on things. I reckon that means I ought to stay in here—"

"Oh, hell," the third man said. "If you two are gonna just stand around and bicker like a couple o' old women, *I'll* go." Hefting his rifle, he strode to the door, opened it, and stalked out into the night. Bagwell went over and closed the door behind him.

That left only two of the outlaws inside the house, and for a moment Fargo considered the possibility that he and Maguire and Terence could jump them and disarm them. The odds would probably never be better.

But there might be gunplay, and the chance was too great that a stray bullet might hit one of the women or the twins. Besides, everything Fargo had said earlier was true: they would all have to fight together to even have a chance of surviving this Indian uprising. The uneasy truce had to stay in place for a while yet.

The man who had gone to the barn didn't come back, and after a while Dewey and Bagwell began to get visibly nervous. "What the hell do you think is takin' Tolbert so long?" Bagwell said.

Dewey shook his head. "I don't know. Maybe I ought to go see if I can find out."

"Hell, no!" Bagwell exclaimed without hesitation. "That'd leave me in here by myself."

"You've got nothin' to fear from us," Maguire rumbled. "We're all on the same side again, remember?"

"Uh-huh," Bagwell said dubiously. "If it's all right with you, mister, I'm stayin' right where I am. And so are you, Dewey."

With a shrug, Dewey agreed. Then he turned quickly toward the door as footsteps sounded on the porch. Both outlaws lifted their rifles.

The door opened, and Nate Hammond stepped into the room. "Stubborn damn bastard," he said without preamble. "He won't talk."

Fargo knew that Hammond was talking about Porter. The boss outlaw went on, "He don't have the loot with him. We searched his saddlebags and the rest of his gear. So he's cached it somewhere. But he won't tell us where, the no-good—"

Dewey finally ran out of patience. He interrupted Hammond, saying, "Nate, is Tolbert still out in the barn?"

Hammond frowned. "Tolbert?" He looked around. "I thought he was in here. Where the hell'd he go?"

"We heard a scream—" Bagwell began.

"That was Porter," Hammond said. "What's that got to do with Tolbert?"

Bagwell pointed at Fargo. "He said that the Paiutes might've come back and grabbed one of you fellas. Said one of us ought to go check."

Hammond swung toward Fargo. "Is that so?" he snapped. "What the hell are you tryin' to pull, Fargo?"

"I'm not trying to pull anything," Fargo replied levelly. "Your friends thought the scream came from the barn, where you were torturing Porter—"

"It did," Hammond cut in.

"And I just pointed out that there might be another explanation for it," Fargo continued. "One of them went to check on it, and that's the last we've seen of him."

Hammond took a step toward Fargo, his hands clenching into fists. "What the hell did you do to Tolbert?" One of those fists lashed out suddenly and slammed into Fargo's jaw, knocking him back off the bench.

Fargo landed hard enough on the puncheon floor that the breath was knocked out of him for a moment. He pushed himself up and rubbed his bearded jaw where Hammond had clouted him.

That was just one more mark against the big outlaw,

Fargo thought. One more score to settle when the time came.

"I didn't do anything to Tolbert," he said. "I've been right here inside the house the whole time."

"He's right about that, Nate," Dewey said. "I've been keeping an eye on him. He couldn't have pulled any sort of trick."

"Then where the hell's Tolbert?" Hammond demanded.

Nobody had an answer for him.

Fargo found himself wondering if the possibility he had suggested earlier was actually true. There could be Paiutes lurking around the relay station. Satonga might have decided it would be better to try to pick off the defenders one by one.

"We'd better take a look around," Fargo said. "And it might be a good idea if we did it together."

Hammond glared at him, but after a few seconds the outlaw nodded. "All right," he said. "But you still ain't gettin' your guns back yet, Fargo."

Hammond told Dewey to stay inside with the women and the twins. The young outlaw didn't argue. Anything that kept him in close proximity to Colleen was going to be all right with Dewey, Fargo thought.

He and Maguire and Terence accompanied Hammond and Bagwell as they left the house, staying in a compact group that bristled with guns. "It ain't all that far to the barn," Hammond said. "What could've happened to Tolbert between here and there?"

"Somebody strike a match," Fargo suggested. "Maybe we can find his footprints and tell something from them."

Bagwell dug out a lucifer and struck it on a boot sole. The flame's glare washed over the ground and revealed a welter of footprints, coming and going.

"Reckon it'll take a real trailsman to make any sense out o' that mess," Hammond said disgustedly.

"You mean like those tracks right there?" Fargo pointed.

Hammond grunted in surprise and leaned over to make a closer study of the marks on the ground that Fargo had indicated. They were long, straight furrows about a foot apart, and they led off at right angles to the course that Tolbert would have followed between the house and the barn.

"What the hell are these?" Hammond asked after a moment.

"I've seen sign like that before," Fargo said. "Those marks were made by the toes of a pair of boots, as a man was being dragged off facedown."

"Tolbert!"

"More than likely," Fargo said. It was looking more and more like his idle speculation had some basis in fact after all.

"Can you follow 'em?"

"I think so."

Fargo led the way toward the wooded slope next to the winding trail that led down from the pass. Bagwell had to strike another couple of matches as they followed the tracks Fargo had found.

As they neared the trees, Terence suddenly said, "Oh, my God, what's *that*?"

Fargo lifted his gaze from the ground and looked toward the junipers. He saw a dark shape standing upright next to one of the tree trunks, unmoving. As the group came closer, Fargo realized that the shape was that of a man who had been tied to the tree.

"I reckon we've found Tolbert," he said.

Hammond muttered a curse and headed quickly for the junipers, followed by Bagwell. Fargo, Maguire, and Terence trailed them at a slightly slower pace. Maguire said to his son, "You might want to stay back, boy. This could be somethin' the likes o' which you've never seen before."

"I'm all right, Pa," Terence insisted, but his voice held a slight tremor.

Fargo knew what to expect, but even so he grimaced when Bagwell struck another match and held it up so that the glare washed over the grisly shape of the man tied to the tree. Fargo recognized him as the outlaw called Tolbert, even though his nose and eyelids had been cut off and a crimson smear of blood covered his face. His trousers had been yanked down and he'd been mutilated. His clumsily hacked-off genitals were stuffed in his mouth, which was wide open in a soundless scream of agony. Fargo had no doubt that Tolbert had still been alive while the mutilation was going on.

He was dead now, though; that was for sure. A small lake of blood had pooled around his feet. Nobody could lose that much blood and still be alive.

"Son of a bitch!" Bagwell exploded. "Look what the bastards done to him!"

Fargo heard the sound of retching behind him and glanced over his shoulder to see that Terence had fallen to hands and knees and was losing the food he had eaten earlier. That wasn't an uncommon reaction for somebody seeing the handiwork of Indians on the warpath for the first time. Fargo had witnessed the results of such atrocities all too many times and was somewhat hardened to them. Despite that, even his stomach felt a little queasy as he looked at what was left of Tolbert.

"Damn it, don't just stand there!" Hammond said raggedly. "Somebody cut him down!"

"I would," Fargo said, "but I don't have my knife, remember?"

Hammond glowered at him. Bagwell stepped forward, drew a knife from a sheath at his waist, and with a hand that shook a little cut the rawhide thongs that lashed Tolbert's body to the juniper. The dead man fell forward when the last of the thongs was severed. Bagwell quickly stepped out of the way so that the blood-soaked corpse wouldn't sag against him.

Hammond rounded angrily on Fargo. "Now there's one less of us to fight off those savages the next time they attack! I blame you for this, Fargo!"

"It was the Paiutes who jumped him and dragged him out here to kill him," Fargo replied. "I didn't have a thing to do with it."

"It was you who put the idea to go out to the barn in his head!"

Fargo didn't bother denying the accusation. "I wasn't trying to get him killed. It occurred to me that some of the Paiutes could be skulking around, that's all. *And they still could be.*"

That obviously true statement made the other men glance around nervously. "We'd best get back to the house," Hammond said.

"What about Tolbert?" Bagwell asked.

"Bring him if you want. It won't make no never-mind to him."

As the men turned back toward the house, Terence struggled to get to his feet. He had only made it to one knee when a pair of shots suddenly blasted through the night.

"Dear Lord, the savages must be tryin' to get in the house!" Maguire burst out. He broke into a run, moving with surprising speed and grace for a big, bulky man.

Hammond and Bagwell were right behind him, leaving Tolbert's corpse where it lay. Callous though it might have been, Hammond's comment was right. Tolbert was far beyond caring what happened now.

Fargo paused to reach down and grasp Terence's arm. He lifted the youngster to his feet. At the same time, Fargo picked up the rifle Terence had dropped on the ground when the sickness hit him. It felt good to have his hand wrapped around a weapon again,

Fargo thought, even though the situation might not last.

He and Terence hurried after the others. No more shots had sounded after the initial pair. As they reached the barn, the two outlaws who were in there with Porter stepped out, clutching their rifles.

Hammond paused long enough to ask, "Did one of you fire those shots?"

"No, Nate, it wasn't us!"

"They came from the house!" the other man added.

"Ava!" Maguire bellowed as he charged toward the house. "Ava, darlin', hang on! I'm comin'!"

"Stay in the barn!" Hammond flung over his shoulders at the two men. "Cover us!"

The outlaws retreated into the barn, rifles raised to their shoulders in case they needed to open fire. The rest of the group ran toward the house, with Maguire in the lead.

The burly stationkeeper slammed the door open and burst through. The others were right behind him. "Ava!" he shouted again.

As Fargo entered the room he saw Ava, Colleen, and the twins huddled next to the stove. They appeared to be all right. Dewey stood at the entrance to the corridor between the sleeping quarters at the back of the big room. The blanket that hung over the opening was swept back, and Dewey had a revolver in his hand, pointed at the rear window. Powder smoke still wisped from the muzzle of the weapon.

"What the hell was the shootin' about?" Hammond demanded.

"I . . . I saw an Indian back there!" Dewey replied. "He was trying to get in the window. I took a couple of shots at him, and then when he disappeared I ran back there and closed the shutters. He might come back, though!"

Hammond scowled. "Are you sure you saw somethin', or did you just imagine there was an Injun tryin' to get in?''

"He was there, I tell you!" Dewey insisted. "I saw him with my own eyes!"

Fargo looked at the wall on both sides of the window and didn't see any marks where bullets had struck it. The insides of the shutters weren't marred, either. That meant the shutters had been open when Dewey fired, and his aim must have been true. The slugs had gone through the open window.

"There's an easy way to find out whether Dewey was imagining things," Fargo pointed out. "Just look around the back of the house and see if you find any tracks or blood from where he shot the Paiute he says he saw."

"I *did* see him, damn it!"

"Yeah, we can check," Hammond said. "Come on." He looked askance at the rifle in Fargo's hands, but he didn't say anything. Fargo thought that a grim realization might be sinking in on the outlaw leader. They might all be fighting for their lives any minute now, with little or no warning.

Hammond told Dewey to stay inside again while the rest of them went around to the rear of the house. "You might as well stay in here, too, boy," he snapped at Terence. "The way you was pukin' your guts up out there, you ain't gonna be much good in a fight."

Fargo thought that was unfair, considering how coolheaded Terence had been during the earlier fracases, but he didn't take the time to argue with Hammond. Instead he followed along as Hammond, Maguire, and Bagwell went out the front door and started around the house.

When they reached the rear corner of the building, Hammond started to say, "I don't see any—" He stopped short and exclaimed, "What the hell!"

They moved closer to the shape lying on the ground

beneath the rear window. Dewey must have heard Hammond's voice, because he called from inside, "Do you see anything out there?"

"Open the shutters," Fargo called in return, and a second later the shutters were pushed back so that light from inside the house spilled on the ground outside the window.

The body of a Paiute warrior lay there, staring sightlessly up at the night sky. There was a red-rimmed black hole in his forehead, just to the left of center. Fargo couldn't see the back of the Indian's head, but he knew it was probably a gory mess where the bullet had blasted out the back of the skull.

"Son of a bitch!" Hammond said. "You really did see a redskin tryin' to get in. And that was mighty good shootin', too. Got him almost right smack between the eyes."

Dewey passed a hand over his face and shuddered a little, which Fargo thought was an odd sort of reaction for a hardened desperado to have after killing a man. He said, "I thought I got him, but I wasn't certain."

"Well, you sure did—".

Before Hammond could say anything else, more shots sounded, this time from the barn. Rifles cracked several times, rapidly, and there was a frantic desperation to the sound.

"Stay in the house!" Hammond snapped at Dewey. "And close them shutters!"

Then he charged back toward the front of the house, followed closely by Fargo, Maguire, and Bagwell.

When the four men rounded the corner and came in sight of the barn, Fargo saw right away that flames were leaping up inside the structure. Dark shapes darted here and there, silhouetted against the hellish glare. Shots spurted from inside the burning barn.

He lifted the rifle to his shoulder and fired without seeming to aim, but one of the scurrying shapes suddenly tumbled head over heels, knocked off its feet by Fargo's bullet.

At the same time, Hammond, Maguire, and Bagwell opened fire at the marauders who had set the barn on fire. The two outlaws who had been left inside the barn emerged then, also shooting at the Paiutes. They fired on the run as they hurried to join Hammond and the others.

"Where's Porter?" bellowed Hammond.

One of the outlaws who had been left to watch the gambler was limping badly where something— probably an arrow—had cut a gash across his thigh. He waved a hand back toward the barn and called over the crackling of flames and the booming of gunfire, "Still in there!"

Fargo was already running toward the barn before the words were out of the man's mouth. Not only had the outlaws abandoned Porter, but they had also left all the animals penned up in their stalls inside the barn, including Fargo's stallion. If they weren't freed they would burn to death, and Fargo wasn't going to let that happen if he could prevent it.

He dashed through the open double doors. Behind him, near the house, Hammond was shouting, "Get Porter! Don't let him die, damn it!"

Fargo didn't know if Hammond was yelling at him or at Bagwell and the other outlaws. Hammond didn't want Porter to die because he hadn't yet found out from the gambler where the stolen loot was cached. Fargo didn't care about that, but he would try to save Porter anyway, just out of human decency.

The Ovaro came first, though.

Flames roared as they consumed straw and wood. Heat pounded at Fargo from both sides as he ran straight to the stall where he had left the stallion. The Ovaro kicked against the stall door, spooked by the smoke and flames. Fargo threw the door open and said, "Get out of here, big fella!" The Ovaro dashed for the outside.

Shots continued to ring out, audible even over the crackling of the blaze. The Paiutes were still out there, and the defenders were fighting a desperate battle against them.

Fargo was fighting a battle of his own, though, and the odds were against him. He didn't know where Porter was, but he looked for the gambler as he ran from stall to stall, opening the doors and setting the Pony Express horses free. They could always be rounded up later—if anybody came through this ruckus alive.

The handful of cows were harder to deal with. The horses all fled on their own once their stalls were open, but the cows had to be driven out. Fargo yelled at them and slapped their rumps with the barrel of the rifle he still held, and finally he got them lumbering toward the open front doors.

He still hadn't found Porter, and there weren't any places left to look except the tack room. Fargo flung open the door to the little room and saw Porter lying on the floor.

Porter was conscious, at least partially, and seemed to be trying to get up, but he lacked the strength. Fargo reached down and grasped his arm, hauling him to his feet. By the light of the flames, he saw that Porter had been beaten even more badly than before. And there were cuts on the man's face where someone had worked on him with the tip of a knife blade.

Hammond, Fargo thought. He had no doubt that the boss outlaw was responsible for this torture.

But there was no time to think about that now. He and Porter had to get out of the barn while they still could. "Come on!" Fargo shouted at Porter, trying to penetrate the stunned lethargy that had the gambler in its grip.

With one hand clamped like iron around Porter's arm, Fargo left the tack room and started toward the entrance. The flames had closed in on both sides of the aisle through the center of the barn. All four walls were burning now, and flames were licking at the roof. The heat was so bad that the world swam dizzily around Fargo as he fought his way toward the doors, dragging Porter with him. Thick smoke clogged the air and stung his eyes and nose and throat fiercely.

The two men stumbled out through the doors into somewhat clearer air, and immediately Fargo felt better. Some of his strength returned. He struggled to get his wits about him again, and as he did, he spotted a shape looming out of the shadows, hurtling toward them.

Fargo let his instincts take over and whirled toward the attacker, lifting the rifle he still clutched as he did so. The barrel blocked the vicious swing of a war ax. Fargo slashed the barrel across the Paiute's face with a backhanded stroke. The front sight opened up a cut in the warrior's face that spurted blood. Fargo struck again, this time slamming the barrel against the Indian's head. The Paiute went down.

The fight had lasted only seconds. Fargo urged Porter toward the house. Hammond, Maguire, and the others had retreated onto the porch. They knelt and crouched there now, guns blasting as they provided covering fire for Fargo and Porter.

They reached the steps and stumbled up them. Fargo practically flung Porter through the open door into the house. He turned to snap a couple of final shots at the Paiutes as he began to back toward the doorway. The other men were retreating, too. One by one they ducked inside. Fargo went through last and yanked the door closed behind him. He heard the *thunk!* as an arrow buried itself in the wood. That had been close.

The defenders crouched at the rifle slits and the partially open shutters, firing out at the Paiutes. The shots began to die away as fewer and fewer targets presented themselves.

"I think they're pullin' back again," Maguire said.

"They've done what they set out to do this time," Fargo said. "They've got us all bunched up in here again, and now, with the barn destroyed and all the horses loose, we couldn't make a run for it even if we wanted to."

"So what happens next?" Hammond asked.

"They keep us bottled up in here while they lick their wounds," Fargo said. "And then, when they decide it's time . . . they overrun the place and kill us, to the last man."

7

The smell of smoke from the burning barn drifted into the house and served as a grim reminder of what had happened. So did the groans of pain from the wounded man as Bagwell poured whiskey on the man's gashed thigh and tied a crude bandage around it.

That was the only injury suffered in the latest attack by the Paiutes, however. If people trapped in their situation could be said to be lucky, Fargo supposed they had been fortunate.

They could have all been dead by now.

The other two outlaws were named Lawson and Ryan. The one with the wounded leg was Ryan. They huddled on one side of the room along with Hammond, Bagwell, and Dewey. Fargo sat with the Maguires at the table on the other side of the room. Porter sat with them, a wet cloth that Ava had given him pressed to his face. The cloth was turning pink from the blood that seeped out of the cuts on Porter's face.

Hammond hadn't demanded that Fargo relinquish the rifle he had picked up just before the fight broke out, nor had he insisted on questioning Porter again about the missing money. Fargo had a feeling that Hammond was finally starting to realize just how bad the situation was. That stolen loot wouldn't be any good to anybody if nobody was left alive to spend it. Tolbert's death and the destruction of the barn seemed to have knocked at least some of the arrogance out of Hammond.

After a while, Fargo stood up and walked deliberately toward the group of outlaws. They watched him tensely. He stopped about halfway across the room and said, "We'd better get men on all the windows, so we'll be ready for the Paiutes when they come again."

"Yeah, I reckon," Hammond said. "Bagwell, you and Lawson take the ones here in front. Dewey, you did such a good job watchin' that back window earlier, you can do that again."

His face pale, Dewey nodded. He still looked disturbed about what had happened when the Paiute tried to get in the rear window. Fargo was unsure why that would bother him, but he was starting to get the glimmering of a possible explanation.

Hammond went on. "Don't think that much has changed, Fargo. I still want that money Porter stole from us, and I still don't trust you. But I reckon we don't have any choice but to get along."

"That's right," Fargo agreed. "Right now we have bigger worries than each other."

Hammond grunted. "Them damn Paiutes."

Maguire spoke up, saying, "There'll be a Pony rider comin' through tomorrow, bound for Salt Lake City. If he can make it, the fella who runs the office there for Russell, Majors, and Waddell will get in touch with the army and let 'em know that we're pinned down here. With any luck we'll have a company o' cavalry campin' on our doorstep in a few days."

Fargo thought Maguire was being overly optimistic. Even if the eastbound Pony rider made it to Salt Lake City, it might take a week or longer to alert the army and get any troops sent to Black Rock Pass. Satonga was probably enjoying tormenting the whites with the uncertainty of when he would attack again, but he wouldn't wait another week to try again to wipe out the defenders. Fargo was convinced of that.

But it wouldn't do any good to say anything like that. If Maguire was just trying to reassure his family, Fargo wasn't going to contradict him. It was better to let them cling to whatever shreds of hope that they could.

And who could say but what they would continue to be lucky? Miracles sometimes happened. . . .

No one felt much like sleeping except the twins, who curled up on pallets on the floor that Ava made for them out of some blankets. Even though to a certain extent they still regarded this whole affair as an adventure, the tension was beginning to get to them, too. Fargo had seen the worry on their faces before they dozed off.

Everyone else planned to sit up the rest of the night, so Ava started a pot of coffee boiling on the stove. When it was ready, she poured cups for her husband and her two oldest children, as well as for Fargo and Porter. Then she said stiffly, "Mr. Hammond, you and your men are welcome to coffee if you want it."

Hammond came over and nodded his thanks. "We're obliged to you, Mrs. Maguire." He took a cup from her, sipped the strong black brew, and nodded in appreciation. "Mighty good, and just what we needed right now."

Even though Hammond was being polite at the moment, Fargo saw the expression in his eyes when he looked at Ava, and he noticed the way Hammond's fingers had deliberately brushed against hers when he took the coffee from her. Fargo was sure that, in the back of Hammond's mind, the outlaw was still thinking that he could ride away from here with not only the money that Porter had stolen from him, but also with Ava and Colleen.

One by one the other men claimed cups of coffee. Dewey carried his back to the chair he had placed by the rear window. Fargo stood up and ambled down the short corridor through the sleeping quarters. Dewey glanced up at him in surprise.

"What do you want, Fargo?"

"Just thought I'd tell you that you did a good job earlier." Fargo sipped from his own cup. "If that Paiute had gotten in here, likely some others would have been right behind him and you and the Maguires would be dead now. You saved those women for sure."

"Well, I . . . I didn't really think about it." Dewey looked uncomfortable. "When I saw him about to climb in, I just jerked my gun up and fired a couple of times. It was just instinct."

"Like Hammond said, that was good shooting."

Dewey shrugged. "Luck."

Fargo ventured a guess. He said, "You never killed anybody before, did you, Dewey?"

"What?" The young outlaw frowned darkly. "Of course I've killed folks before. I . . . I shot a bunch of times at those Paiutes when they were chasing us."

"But you don't *know* that your shots hit any of them," Fargo said quietly. "That's a little different than looking at a dead man and knowing that his life is over because *you* pulled a trigger. Knowing that they have that much power in their hands makes some men feel like . . . well, like God, I suppose." Fargo paused. "Others it just makes them feel like the devil."

Dewey shook his head stubbornly. "I don't know what you're talking about." The look in his eyes told Fargo a different story, though. It said that Fargo had guessed right about the Paiute.

"Whatever you say." Fargo shrugged. "It just seems to me that a fella like you ought to be a little more careful about the company he keeps. When you ride with a man like Hammond, you might wind up doing some things you'd rather not do."

The coffee cup shook a little in Dewey's hand. "Go on back out there and sit down with the Maguires, Fargo. You shouldn't be back here bothering me while I'm trying to stand guard."

"Yeah, I reckon you're right." Fargo turned and went back to the main room, satisfied that at least he had planted a seed in Dewey's mind. The young outlaw was smitten with Colleen Maguire Ashe. Maybe, if a final showdown came and Hammond tried to carry through on his plan to kidnap the two women, Dewey would try to stop him.

It was a slim chance, but Fargo's adventurous life had long since taught him that slim chances were a hell of a lot better than none.

Hammond glared at him suspiciously when he returned to the table. He was probably wondering what Fargo had been doing, talking to Dewey. Fargo halfway expected Hammond to go talk to Dewey himself, but the boss outlaw stayed where he was, in a chair near the fireplace. Hammond probably believed that his hold on his men was secure. Maybe it was.

The night continued to drag past. Minutes stretched out painfully. Fargo decided that if the Paiutes were going to attack again, it would be at dawn, when the defenders' spirits would be at their lowest ebb.

Dawn arrived uneventfully, though. The sun rose over the Cricket Range to the east and slanted its red rays through Black Rock Pass. Despite their best intentions, the people inside the relay station dozed. Exhaustion even caught up with Fargo, two near-sleepless nights in a row taking their toll even on his iron constitution. His head sagged forward onto his crossed arms, which were resting on the table.

He came awake with a sudden jerk, thinking that something was wrong. The room was quiet, though, except for some snores that came from one of the outlaws who was stretched out on the floor in front of the fireplace. Fargo blinked and stared around the room. Ava was already at the stove, cooking some bacon. She looked at Fargo and smiled.

He nodded a good morning to her and got to his feet. Several of the others were stirring as well. Fargo tucked the rifle under his arm and walked toward the door. Hammond started up out of the rocker where he had been dozing and demanded, "Where the hell do you think you're goin'?"

"To take a look around," Fargo replied. "The sun's up. The Paiutes will be less likely to attack now."

"Those redskins will fight in the daylight. Don't think they won't."

"I know that." Some people insisted that Indians would never attack at night, while others held the exact opposite belief. The truth was, Fargo knew, that Indians attacked whenever they thought they had the best chance of winning, and that might be any hour of the day or night.

Satonga seemed to have a preference for attacking while it was dark, though, at least based on the experiences of the past two nights. That made Fargo think it was reasonably safe to take a quick look outside.

He did so, swinging the door open. His mouth quirked in a wry smile at the sight of half a dozen arrows sticking in the door. More arrows protruded from the logs of the house's front wall. The Paiutes had peppered the place with their shafts, hoping to send one of them through a rifle slit and into the eye of one of the defenders. Such long shots had been known to happen.

Fargo didn't see any bodies of fallen warriors. Again, their comrades had recovered them so that they could be laid to rest with the proper rituals.

The barn was a smoking, blackened heap of ruins

and rubble. The house was set far enough apart from it so that there hadn't been much danger of the fire spreading from one building to the other. The fact that the Paiutes hadn't attempted to burn the house yet still puzzled Fargo.

Maybe Satonga wanted to loot the place before he destroyed it. That made sense, Fargo reflected. Satonga would know that he could find plenty of guns and ammunition inside the house. If the whole Paiute nation was rising against the whites, arming his band with repeaters and plenty of bullets would be a considerable triumph for the war chief. That had to be the answer.

Fargo didn't see any of the horses he had freed from the blazing barn the night before, but the cattle were grazing on the hillside just above the relay station. They wouldn't wander far. He let out a shrill whistle and wasn't surprised when he saw the Ovaro emerge from the junipers. The big stallion gave a toss of his head and trotted toward Fargo.

The Trailsman smiled as the Ovaro came up to him. He patted the horse's shoulder and said, "I figured you'd be somewhere around here, old boy. Are you all right?"

Quickly, he checked the Ovaro and found that the stallion was unhurt. The horse followed him back to the porch.

Sam Maguire came out of the house, stretching and yawning. He looked at the ruins of the barn and shook his head sadly. "I hate to see such a thing, but I suppose a barn can always be rebuilt. Do you know where the other horses are?"

Fargo shook his head and pointed at the hill. "My stallion was up there in the trees, and I wouldn't be surprised if the others are, too."

Maguire rubbed his jaw. "I'll need a fresh mount for that Pony rider comin' through. . . ."

"I can ride up there and see if I can round up some of them," Fargo offered.

"Yeah, and you might be ridin' right into a Paiute trap, too."

"There's that to consider."

Maguire got a thoughtful look on his face and said, "You know, Fargo, if there's any man alive who could get on his horse right now and make it through them Paiutes alive, I reckon it'd be you."

"I told you before, Sam, I'm not going to abandon you."

"But if you could send help back—"

"It might be too late," Fargo said. He shook his head. "We're in this together, and we're going to stay that way."

"Well, you're a good friend, Skye Fargo, that's all I've got to say. I just hope you're not bein' a damn fool by stickin' with us."

Maguire went back in the house, and a moment later Hammond stepped out. The outlaw still had a suspicious look on his face. "What sort of mischief were you and Maguire hatchin' up, Fargo?" he asked.

"No mischief. Can't you get it through your head, Hammond, that we can't be working against each other now?"

"Just don't forget who's runnin' this show," Hammond said with a dark scowl. He turned and stalked back inside.

Fargo laughed softly. The thing of it was, Hammond *wasn't* running things anymore. Satonga was. And knowing that had to be eating at the outlaw.

Fargo turned his head and looked up at the mountains. As he had several times before, he felt the eyes of the Paiutes on him. Somewhat mockingly, he raised his hand to the brim of his hat in a wry salute.

The door opened again, and this time it was Colleen

who stepped outside. She carried a couple of empty buckets.

"Walk with me to the well, Skye?" she asked.

"I don't know if you should be getting that far away from the house," Fargo said.

"You've been looking around. Have you seen any Paiutes this morning?"

"No, but that doesn't mean they're not out there. There could be fifty of them within bowshot right now."

"We need water. Ma wants to keep several days' supply on hand, just in case things get bad enough we can't get out at all. I volunteered to fill up the barrels."

That actually wasn't a bad idea, Fargo thought. "Let's do this as quick as we can," he said.

Side by side, they walked briskly toward the well, which was close to what remained of the barn. Fargo's eyes moved constantly, scanning the landscape all around, and the rifle was ready for instant use in his hands. When they got there, Colleen hooked one of the buckets to the windlass and lowered it.

She filled both buckets, but instead of starting back to the house with them, she set them on the ground at her feet and said, "Skye, I've been thinking about what happened in the barn a couple of nights ago."

"That was mighty nice, all right," Fargo agreed.

"I wish it could happen again."

"Well . . . I don't reckon this is hardly the time or place—"

"I know that. But . . . there are no windows on this side of the house. Nobody could see us if we sort of . . . stole a little kiss."

She moved closer to Fargo as she spoke, close enough so that she could lift a hand and rest it on his chest. She was a tall girl and didn't have to tilt her head back too far in order to be able to look into his lake blue eyes.

Fargo smiled at her. She was right: in desperate circumstances such as these, they had to steal whatever good moments they could.

He leaned over her and brought his mouth down on hers.

Colleen moved against him and brought her arms up around his neck. He still had the rifle in one hand, but he pressed the other hand to her back. Her lips opened boldly, and her tongue was equally daring as it slipped into his mouth and darted sensuously around his.

Fargo responded to the softness of her belly pressed against his groin. He began to harden as she molded herself even tighter to him. Passion swelled in both of them, and they were slightly breathless when they broke the kiss at last.

"There," Colleen said in some satisfaction. "Now we've both got a good reason to survive this damned ordeal."

Fargo already planned on surviving if at all possible, but he didn't point that out. Instead he just smiled and rubbed the small of her back. That made her close her eyes and utter a small sound of contentment.

"Hey!" The sudden, unexpected shout from the direction of the house made them both jump. "Hey, what the hell!"

Fargo let go of Colleen and stepped to the side so that he could see past her. Dewey jumped down from the end of the porch and walked stiffly but rapidly toward them.

"What in blazes do you think you're doing, Fargo?" he demanded as he came closer.

"This is none of your business, Dewey—" Fargo began.

"The hell it's not!" the young outlaw shouted, and with that he launched himself at Fargo, swinging a fist wildly at the Trailsman's head.

Colleen let out a frightened, startled cry as she leaped back to get out of the way. Fargo ducked and let Dewey's punch whistle harmlessly over his head. He put his free hand on Dewey's chest and gave him a hard shove that sent him staggering back several steps.

"Let it go, Dewey," Fargo advised in a hard voice. "This is a fight that neither of us need right now."

"Yeah, you'd like that," Dewey said, almost panting from the anger that had him in its grip. "You just want to keep Colleen all to yourself, instead of giving anybody else a chance with her."

Colleen stared at him. "Have you lost your mind?" she said. "You and your friends come in here and run roughshod over everybody and act like you own the place, and . . . and you think there's any chance that I'd ever *like* you?"

"Don't say that!" Dewey implored her. "I'm not like the others, Colleen. Yeah, I've been riding with them, but I . . . I'm not really like them, I swear it. And no matter what happens, I'd never let any of them hurt you or your family. Not Nate, and not any of the others."

From behind him, Hammond drawled, "Well, now, ain't this a mighty interestin' turn of events?" He cocked the revolver that he brought up. "Are you turnin' on your pards, Dewey, just like that bastard Porter did? Well, now, are you?"

Fargo had seen Hammond coming from the house but hadn't had time to say anything to warn Dewey. Anyway, the young man was so caught up in jealousy and anger that he probably wouldn't have heeded anything Fargo had to say.

But now things were out in the open, and Fargo

didn't know what this sudden fracture in the gang was going to mean.

Dewey half turned toward Hammond. "Nate, I didn't mean I was turning on you. You know I wouldn't do that. But I don't see any reason to hurt these folks—"

"I do the thinkin' in this bunch," Hammond said coldly. "You know that. I give the orders, too, and if you don't want to take 'em, you know what that means." He lowered the hammer on his gun and slid the iron back into leather. Then, with a savage grin on his face, he stood there poised to draw again and said, "Go right ahead, Dewey, if that's what you want."

For a long moment Dewey didn't move or say anything. Then he shook his head and said, "You know that's not what I want, Nate. You and the boys have been good friends to me. I'll stick with you."

Hammond's grin became one of self-satisfaction. "I sort of thought you would, Dewey. Now get back in the house." He jerked a thumb over his shoulder at the building behind him.

Dewey shuffled in that direction. Hammond stood aside, giving him plenty of room. It was obvious to Fargo that Hammond didn't fully trust the young outlaw now, no matter what Dewey had said.

Hammond looked at Fargo and Colleen and said, "Finish whatever you're doin' and get back in the house. You don't want them Paiutes to catch you out here in the open."

"I've been keeping an eye out for them," Fargo said.

"Well, they're tricky bastards, those redskins. You ought to know that."

Fargo nodded. He picked up one of the full water buckets and said to Colleen, "Let's take these in and dump them in the barrels."

She caught her bottom lip between her teeth and nodded, clearly still disturbed by everything that had happened.

For the next half hour, Fargo and Colleen trooped back and forth between the house and the well, using the buckets to fill the water barrels inside the house. Hammond stood at the end of the porch, thumbs hooked in his gun belt, watching them.

Dewey was back at the rear window, Fargo noted while he and Colleen were inside. He didn't look at them as they came in, dumped the water buckets in the barrels, and then went out again.

The young outlaw was probably embarrassed, Fargo thought, not only because he had blurted out his feelings for Colleen but because Hammond had cowed him so easily. Something like that would gnaw on the guts of a proud young man. Fargo still held out some hope that if Hammond and the other outlaws tried to harm the Maguires, Dewey might turn on them.

Once the water barrels were full, Fargo approached Sam Maguire and asked, "When's that eastbound rider due?"

"Two o'clock this afternoon," the stationkeeper replied. "If he makes it through all the Paiutes west of here."

"He's got a better chance of doing that, since the terrain favors the man on the faster horse." Fargo shook his head. "I don't know if he can get through the pass, though. He won't be able to keep his horse at a gallop, and there are plenty of places for the Indians to hide."

"What are you sayin', Fargo?"

"That we owe it to this young man, whoever he is, to let him know that the odds will be against him if he continues his run. He might be better off staying here with us."

With a frown, Maguire said, "That would mean that

the Pony Express has come to a dead stop in both directions . . . and at my station. That's a bad thing for a man to have on his reputation, Fargo.''

"I don't see how anybody could blame you, Sam. You didn't make the Paiutes go on the warpath.''

"No, but I'm responsible for seein' that the mail goes through along this stretch,'' Maguire insisted. He sighed. "Still, I see what you mean. All the Pony riders are almost like my own sons. I can't send one of them into such danger without makin' sure he knows what he's gettin' into.''

"That's all I'm suggesting,'' Fargo said. "The rider will have to make up his own mind whether he wants to stay here or go on.''

"He can't go on without a fresh horse,'' Maguire said as he scratched his jaw in thought. "The mount he's on will be wore out.''

"And I can't rustle up one of the horses that I freed from the barn without riding up into the hills and risking my neck.''

"Well, hell,'' Maguire rumbled. "Looks like that sort of solves our problem for us, don't it? Gives us one more man to help defend the place. But then there's no chance of gettin' word to the army of how bad we're pinned down.''

Keeping his voice quiet so that only Maguire could hear, Fargo said, "There wasn't much chance of that anyway, Sam, at least not of the army getting here in time to help.''

Maguire sighed again. "I know. This is a fight we can't win, isn't it, Fargo?''

"You never know,'' Fargo said. "Stranger things have happened.''

Maguire snorted. "I'd like to see *that*.''

Time inched by. Ava prepared a pot of stew for the midday meal, although no one had much of an appetite. Everyone's nerves were stretched almost to the

107

breaking point. The outlaws took turns standing guard, and several times during the day one of them called out, saying that he had seen something, but on each occasion it proved to be nothing. The false alarms just added to everyone's tension, though.

Two o'clock came and went, and Fargo said to Maguire, "That rider is running late." He left unspoken the thought that the delay might mean bad news, but Maguire knew that anyway.

They stepped out onto the porch and looked to the west, across the arid flats that stretched all the way to the Nevada border. Their eyes searched that vast expanse for a column of dust that might mark the location of the Pony rider. Neither Fargo nor Maguire saw anything promising.

"He didn't even make it this far," Maguire said in a gloomy voice.

"Maybe something happened to delay him somewhere along the line," Fargo suggested. "We can't be sure yet."

They went back in the house. Ava looked at them questioningly, and Maguire just shook his head.

About an hour later, though, as Fargo sat at the table, he lifted his head suddenly when his keen ears picked up the distant drumming of hoofbeats. "Somebody's coming," he announced as he got to his feet. By the time he reached the door, Maguire was right behind him, followed by Terence, Hammond, and Bagwell. The five of them crowded out onto the porch.

This time Fargo had no trouble seeing the cloud of dust to the west. It moved steadily closer, and after a few minutes he could make out a small dark shape at the base of it. As the dust came even closer, that shape resolved itself into the figure of a galloping horse with a rider on top of it, bent far forward in the saddle.

"Maybe he'll have news," Maguire said hopefully. "Maybe the army's already on their way out here."

Fargo didn't hold out much hope of that, but he found himself eager for the rider's arrival, too.

Then, as the lathered horse raced nearer and nearer, a feeling of dread took hold of Fargo. He didn't like the way the rider was swaying back and forth slightly in the saddle. That unsteadiness could have been caused by exhaustion—or it might be because of something else.

When the horse galloped up to the relay station, Fargo's fears were realized. He saw two arrows sticking up from the rider's back. The young man was either dead or unconscious, because he made no move to rein his mount to a halt. Fargo ran out in front of the horse, jerked his hat off his head, and waved it in the air as he yelled. The horse shied violently, and that pitched the rider out of the saddle. He landed hard, without attempting to break his fall.

Once the weight was off the saddle, the exhausted horse came to a stop. Fargo hurried past the animal and dropped to a knee next to the fallen rider. Maguire and Terence rushed up behind him, while Hammond and Bagwell stayed on the porch.

"Is he—" Maguire began.

"Dead," Fargo confirmed grimly. "I'm not sure how he managed to hang on this long, with those two arrows in him."

"That's Jimmy Cordie," Terence said in a choked voice. "He . . . he was stubborn. Proud of how he always got the mail pouch through, no matter what."

Maguire took the pouch off the saddle. "Well, he got it through again, the poor lad. He just won't be carryin' it on from here."

Fargo stood up. "We'll bury him next to Billy Conners. We ought to get those two outlaws who were killed into the ground, too." He frowned. "With the mail pouches stopped both east and west, the folks at the other stations have to be wondering what's going on out here. Maybe the army *is* on its way."

"But it'll take time for any troops to get here," Maguire said.

Fargo nodded, his face bleak as he looked down at the arrow-riddled corpse of the young Pony Express rider. "And until they do—if they do—we're on our own."

8

All the other men stood guard while Fargo and Terence dug three more graves. There was no service this time, as there had been for Billy Conners. They didn't have any canvas to wrap the bodies, so Ava provided blankets, and as soon as the holes were deep enough, the shrouded shapes were lowered into them and the graves were refilled. Then everyone went inside quickly to continue watching for the Paiutes.

By nightfall, the feeling of impending doom had grown stronger in Fargo. He wasn't the sort of man to ever give up hope, but he was also practical enough to realize just how bad their situation really was. Satonga would be running out of patience. Tonight, it was likely that he would attack the Black Rock Pass relay station with every warrior at his command.

After supper, which again no one felt much like eating, Hammond came over to the table and said to the gambler, "Listen, Porter, you might as well tell me what you did with our money. Hell, none of us are gettin' out of here alive anyway, so indulge my curiosity, why don't you?"

Porter just looked up coldly at him and said, "Go to hell, Nate. I want you to die knowing that I beat you."

For a second Fargo thought that Hammond was going to reach for his gun. He was ready to move if the outlaw tried it. But Hammond just glared at Porter for a moment and then said, "You didn't win nothin'. You're gonna be just as dead as the rest of us."

"But I'll die a rich man," Porter said with a smile. He winced as the expression made the ugly cuts on his face hurt.

Hammond turned and stalked angrily back to the other side of the room. He snapped at Bagwell and Lawson to stay alert as they watched at the windows.

Maguire sat down next to Fargo and leaned close to him to say in a low voice, "They'll be comin' tonight, the whole bunch of 'em. You feel it, too, don't you, Fargo?"

Fargo nodded. "I think you're right, Sam."

"I'm givin' pistols to Ava and Colleen, with instructions for 'em to save a couple o' rounds in each one. A bullet each for Matt and Pat, and . . . and one for themselves."

"Maybe it won't come to that," Fargo said. Still, he thought, it was a sensible precaution for Maguire to take.

Fargo was sitting at the table with the Maguires, sipping from a cup of coffee, when he saw Dewey emerge from the corridor at the rear of the room. The young outlaw said to Ryan, "Go back there and keep an eye on that window."

Ryan hadn't stood guard very much because of his wounded leg, and he didn't want to now. He grumbled, "You don't give the orders around here, kid. Nate does."

"I know that. Do it as a favor to me."

"And why in the hell would I want to do you a favor?"

Hammond spoke up from one of the rocking chairs. "Stop grousin', Ryan, and do what Dewey asked you to. The kid's got something on his mind, and I want to know what it is."

Still complaining under his breath, Ryan got up and

limped down the corridor to the rear window. Dewey took a deep breath and approached the table.

"Colleen," he said, "I've got something I want to tell you."

Sam Maguire frowned. "I'm not sure you got anything to say that my daughter would be interested in, mister."

"No offense, sir, but I got to get this out."

Hammond put in, "Let him talk, Maguire. I'm interested in what he's got to say, whether you and the girl are or not."

Maguire shrugged his broad shoulders. "Can't stop a man from talkin', I reckon."

"Thanks." Dewey faced Colleen, who lifted her head and defiantly met his intense gaze. He swallowed hard, obviously nervous, and said, "I know you think I'm just a no-good outlaw like the rest o' this bunch—"

"Hey!" Bagwell said indignantly. Hammond made a motion for him to be quiet.

Dewey went on, "But the truth is, I've only been riding with them for a month or so, and I wasn't a part of any of the jobs they pulled before that."

"Careful, Dewey," Hammond cautioned, and Fargo silently echoed that. He didn't want Dewey getting too specific about some of the things Hammond and the others had done in the past, because then Hammond might feel like he *had* to kill the Maguires—if by some chance they all lived through this night.

"None of what happened before matters," Dewey said, "leastways not to me, because I wasn't part of it. Porter didn't steal any loot from me. He'd already left the bunch long before I ever met them. So if you think I'm like them, you're wrong." He gave Colleen a curt nod. "I just wanted you to know that."

Her face was pale but resolute. "You're with them now," she said. "I don't see that you're any different."

"Well . . . if the Paiutes don't get us all, you will see. Because I don't intend to ride with them anymore."

"Don't be a damn fool, Dewey," Hammond said harshly. "Don't let a pretty face muddle your mind. You know that if you stick with us, you'll come through this all right, and sooner or later you'll be a rich man."

Dewey turned toward the boss outlaw. "I don't care about that. Nate, don't you see that I'm not cut out to be like you and the others? Why, I'd be happier staying here and helping Mr. Maguire rebuild the barn and run the relay station!"

Maguire said dryly, "I don't recall offerin' you a job, mister."

"I'm just saying that's something I'd like to do." Dewey looked at Colleen again. "Something I'd really like to do."

"Well, it's good to know that you'd turn on old friends like that," Hammond said. "I reckon I was right not to trust you, Dewey."

The young man looked over his shoulder. "You don't have to feel that way, Nate. Can't we just . . . come to a parting of the ways?"

Hammond came slowly to his feet. "When somebody rides with me, they don't cross me. Not ever."

Porter laughed and said, "At least not often."

"Shut up! You don't look to me like it worked out all that well for you, Porter."

The gambler shrugged. "I'm alive . . . and you don't have your money. I'm satisfied so far."

Hammond took a step toward the table. Fargo stood up and moved so that he was between the outlaw and the Maguires. "That's enough," he said. "You can all fight your personal battles when this is over."

Hammond glared at him. "I won't forget any of this. There'll be plenty of scores to settle—"

"Help!" Ryan shouted from the rear window. "Help! Paiutes!" His gun roared.

114

Earlier, Fargo had reclaimed his own Henry and Colt, along with the Arkansas toothpick, and given Terence back the rifle he had been carrying. Hammond hadn't objected. Now Fargo snatched up the Henry from the table where he had placed it and dashed to the opening. He saw Ryan staggering back, the head of a war ax buried in his shoulder. The Paiute warrior who had struck him with the weapon loomed in the window.

Fargo fired the Henry in a snap shot, but instinct and experience guided the bullet. It struck the Paiute in the chest and drove him back out of the window. Another warrior sprang to take his place, but that one caught a slug in the face from Fargo's Henry and tumbled back out of sight, too.

Fargo ran past the slumping Ryan, slammed the shutters closed, and dropped the bar that would hold them in place. At the same time, shots began to ring out in the main room, and Fargo heard Bagwell shout, "They're all over the place."

Like the Texians who had been trapped in the Alamo, the defenders of the Black Rock Pass relay station were surrounded. Fargo jerked Ryan upright. The ax was in the outlaw's left shoulder, and Ryan still held a revolver in his right hand. "Can you use that gun?" Fargo asked him.

Ryan propped his back against one of the beams that held up the roof and nodded weakly. "Go on, Fargo," he said. "Any of the damn redskins try to get in back here, I'll give 'em a hot lead welcome!"

Fargo believed Ryan. His whining and complaining were forgotten. Outlaw or not, like most frontiersmen he had a core of inner strength that came to the forefront when he was confronted by danger. He would hold out against the Paiutes as long as he could.

But he was losing quite a bit of blood from that shoulder wound and would probably pass out sooner or later. For now, though, Fargo had no choice but to trust him.

Fargo wheeled around and hurried back into the main room. Maguire, Terence, Hammond, Dewey, Bagwell, and Lawson were all at rifle slits, keeping up a steady fire. At the table, Colleen and Ava loaded the extra rifles, and the twins ran back and forth between the defensive positions, delivering loaded weapons and taking empty ones back to the table to be reloaded. Everyone seemed to be working calmly and efficiently.

Stepping over to one of the empty rifle slits, Fargo thrust the barrel of the Henry through the narrow opening between logs and drew a quick bead on one of the shadowy figures darting in front of the house. He pulled the trigger but couldn't tell if he hit the Paiute or not. Working the rifle's lever, he waited for another target.

Something slammed against the door, probably the trunk of a juniper hauled down from the mountains. "They're tryin' to break in!" Maguire yelled unnecessarily. The battering ram crashed against the door a second time, but the thick beam that served as a bar continued to hold.

Fargo angled the barrel of his rifle as much as he could, but he couldn't bring it around far enough to reach the Paiutes using the battering ram. It was a desperate situation, and that called for desperate measures to meet it.

Fargo turned away from the rifle slit and ran into the rear corridor again. Ryan still stood there, lines of pain etched on his unshaven face.

"Hasn't been any more of 'em tryin' to get in back here," he said in a thin voice.

"Good," Fargo said, "because I'm going out this way."

Ryan's eyes widened in shock. "You're goin' out there amongst them howlin' savages?"

Fargo jerked his head in a nod. "Bar the window again after me."

He threw the bar up and swung the shutters in, halfway expecting to see the hate-contorted face of a Paiute warrior staring at him from the opening.

But there was no one out there at the moment. Fargo climbed out quickly, leaving the Henry behind. He would have to rely on his Colt for the work that faced him now.

He drew the gun as he dashed to the nearest corner of the building. Behind him, Ryan slammed the shutters as Fargo had instructed. Fargo glanced around the corner and saw plenty of Paiutes firing arrows and rifles at the house, but for the moment they were concentrating their fire on the front of the building.

He holstered the Colt, turned to the wall, and began to climb.

The logs and rocks of which the house was constructed offered enough handholds and toeholds so that Fargo was able to climb right up the wall. When he reached the overhang of the roof it became more difficult. He had to lean back a little, grasp the edge of the roof, and then let his legs dangle while he pulled himself up by the sheer strength of his arms. He grunted with the effort as his muscles strained against his weight. After what seemed like ages but was probably only a handful of seconds, he was high enough so that he could kick a leg up onto the roof. A couple of heartbeats later he rolled onto the logs that formed the roof.

Fargo drew the Colt again as he came up in a crouch and duckwalked toward the roof's peak. Below him, the yelling and shooting continued in a bloodcurdling racket. He heard the battering ram strike the door for at least the third time.

Then he topped the crest, stretched out on his stomach, and crawled down onto the porch overhang. The

Indians seemed to have no idea he was there, but that was about to change. When he reached the edge, he took his hat off, stuck his head and his gun arm off the porch, and with his head hanging upside down he emptied the Colt, blasting a hail of bullets into the Paiutes who held the juniper trunk ready to smash against the door again.

The storm of lead scythed through the warriors. The battering ram dropped heavily to the porch as the men holding it fell to Fargo's deadly shots. The Paiutes were taken completely by surprise, and Fargo pulled back and rolled away from the edge so quickly that some of the Indians must have wondered where those unexpected shots had come from.

Other warriors realized he was up here, though, and that would make him a sitting duck if he didn't move fast. He rolled over, came up on hands and knees, and scrambled for the thick stone chimney that rose from the roof at one end of the building. Arrows cut through the air around his head. He reached the chimney and threw himself behind it. Pressing his back against the stone column, he began reloading the Colt as quickly as he could, his movements swift and sure from long practice.

Where he was now, the house itself shielded him to a large extent, and as several of the Paiutes tried to circle the building and get at him that way, he fired down into their midst and sent a couple of the warriors tumbling off their feet. The others yelled their outrage and pulled back.

Fargo's lips curved in a grim smile. He had the high ground, so to speak, but could he hold it?

A sudden flare of light caught his attention. He risked a look around the chimney and spotted one of the warriors about fifty yards away, drawing back a bowstring on which a flaming arrow was nocked. No matter how much Satonga wanted to capture the relay station without destroying it so that he could loot the place of its weapons, the war chief had to be getting frustrated with the stubborn defenders. Now he was prepared to try to burn them out.

It was a mighty long shot for a handgun, and Fargo had only a split second to react before the Paiute launched the blazing missile. The Colt came up and roared as it bucked against the palm of Fargo's hand.

He barely seemed to aim, but the Paiute was driven backward by the bullet just as he released the bowstring. Since he had been falling as he let the arrow fly, it went up into the air in a much steeper arc than the warrior had intended. The blazing brand seemed to light up the sky for a second as it rose, then reached its peak and curved back to earth well short of the house, its intended target.

Several more Paiutes rushed forward with flaming arrows, but the defenders in the house had been alerted to this new menace, and a volley of shots blasted out to cut down the Indians before they could fire. The arrows that fell to the ground continued to burn, casting a garish light over the area in front of the house.

Fargo saw a Paiute on horseback ride into that hellish glare, waving a rifle over his head and screaming at the other warriors to urge them on. Even though Fargo had never laid eyes on the man before, his instincts told him he was looking at Satonga at last. The feathered headdress and the proud, furious, hawklike face identified the war chief, along with the distinctive markings on his buckskins. Satonga's rage and frustration had driven him to take a hand personally in this attack.

Fargo had hoped that Satonga would be drawn into the battle. The war chief's arrival on the scene gave the Trailsman the opportunity to take the biggest gamble of all. . . .

He holstered the Colt, drew the Arkansas toothpick from the sheath on his calf, and went down the front slope of the roof at a run. Satonga didn't see Fargo coming until it was too late. Fargo launched himself off the roof in a dive that sent him crashing into the Paiute leader. The impact of the collision drove Satonga off his pony.

Both men slammed into the ground, but Satonga was on the bottom and took the brunt of the fall. The other Paiutes were so surprised to see their war chief brought low that they broke off the attack momentarily. The defenders inside the house took advantage of the opportunity to pour more gunfire into them. Several of the warriors caught out in the open fell to the flying lead.

Fargo's arm came up as he lifted the big knife, then slashed down in what he intended to be a killing stroke. Even stunned, though, Satonga was a magnificent fighter. His hand shot up and grabbed Fargo's wrist, stopping the blade before it could land. Satonga grunted with the effort of holding off the knife.

Fargo levered himself up with his other arm and then brought that fist across in a crashing blow to Satonga's jaw that rocked the war chief's head to the side. Satonga's grip on Fargo's wrist didn't ease, though. Instead he rolled and heaved and twisted, and Fargo found himself being thrown off to the side.

He might have been able to shoot Satonga from the roof, but he knew how much more demoralizing it would be to the Paiutes if he defeated the war chief in hand-to-hand combat. Knowing the way they thought, he had realized that if he killed Satonga, the other Paiutes might believe that they had lost their medicine and would abandon the attack on the relay station. Fargo knew those were long odds, but at the same time, this was the best chance he had to save the Maguire family.

Satonga came after him, just as Fargo expected. He got a foot up and drove the heel of his boot into the war chief's belly. Satonga's breath was knocked out of him in a foul gust. Fargo swung his leg even higher and sent the Paiute leader flying over his head.

Fargo rolled over and was up almost before Satonga crashed to the ground. Satonga recovered almost as quickly, though, and came up slashing with a war ax that he had taken from behind the rawhide belt around his waist. Fargo had to give ground before the attack, backing away rapidly. Satonga rushed after him, howling savagely.

Fargo was vaguely aware that the shooting had stopped on both sides. Everyone was watching this desperate battle between the two men as they surged back and forth in the flickering light from the guttering fire arrows. It was as if they all sensed, white and red alike, that the real outcome of this battle would be determined by the epic struggle between Fargo and Satonga.

As the war ax whistled over his head, Fargo ducked under the slashing blow and launched himself in another diving tackle. His arms went around Satonga's hips. The war chief was knocked backward off his feet. Fargo felt the war ax strike the back of his left leg. It was the flat of the ax head that caught him, not the keen edge, so it didn't bite into muscle and bone. Still, the blow had enough force behind it to make Fargo's leg go numb for a moment.

Fargo got his left hand on Satonga's right wrist as the war chief lifted the ax for another blow. Satonga grabbed the wrist of Fargo's knife hand. They were locked together on the ground, each straining to hold off the other's weapon, their faces only inches apart. Fargo saw the hatred blazing in Satonga's eyes. The war chief's headdress had come off during the struggle, and the scent of the rancid grease that he rubbed on his hair sickened Fargo a little. He ignored that, though, and concentrated on the life-or-death conflict.

The two men were so evenly matched that the wild thought that they might still be here a hundred years from now, straining against each other, went crazily through Fargo's head. But then Satonga's grip slipped a little, and for the first time Fargo saw a glimmer of panic in the war chief's eyes.

But Fargo realized almost instantly that it was a trick. Satonga was trying to get him to pour all his effort into his knife arm, which would mean that Fargo would relax his grip a little on the wrist of the hand holding the ax.

Fargo didn't fall for it. Instead he threw his weight against Satonga's right arm, driving it out and down and smashing the wrist against a rock that lay on the ground beside them.

Satonga cried out in pain and anger as the ax slipped out of his fingers, and this time when his grip on Fargo's wrist slipped, it was the real thing. The muscles in Fargo's shoulders bunched as he drove the Arkansas toothpick into Satonga's chest. The razor-sharp blade grated on bone, sliced through muscle, and then reached the war chief's heart. Satonga's back arched up off the ground as his heels drummed spasmodically against the dirt. Rage and disbelief kept the life in his eyes for a second or two, but then it faded.

Satonga was dead. Fargo had killed him even though he had never even seen the man until a few minutes earlier. There was no personal enmity between them. Fate had simply cast them on different sides in a war, a war not of Fargo's choosing. He had never hated Satonga—but he hoped the war chief's death brought about an end to this fight.

Fargo sat up and pulled the Arkansas toothpick from the Paiute leader's body. An eerie silence hung over the relay station and the area around it. Fargo saw dozens of Paiute warriors and hoped that the defenders inside the house had the sense not to shoot. That would just start the battle up all over again.

Silence continued to reign as Fargo pushed himself to his feet. He didn't know if any of the Paiutes spoke English or not, but he said in a loud voice anyway, "Your leader is dead. He met his death nobly, one warrior striving against another. This fight is over."

All but one of the fire arrows had burned out, but in the light of the remaining brand, Fargo saw one of the Paiutes step forward. The man came toward him deliberately. Fargo moved back, also deliberately, away from Satonga's body. Several more warriors followed the first one. He gestured at Satonga, and the others bent and picked up the fallen war chief to bear him away into the darkness. Then the Paiute warrior who had given the order looked at Fargo for a long moment before nodding his head curtly.

Fargo knew what that meant, even before the warrior turned and stalked away after the others.

It was over.

During the next few minutes, all the Paiutes faded off into the night. Fargo stood there, out in the open, until they were gone. Then he wiped Satonga's blood from the blade of the Arkansas toothpick on the leg of his buckskin trousers and slid the big knife back in its sheath. He turned toward the house.

The door was thrown open before Fargo got there. Sam Maguire rushed out, followed by Terence. "You did it!" he shouted in happy disbelief at Fargo. "You drove them away, and I don't reckon they'll come back this time!"

Fargo smiled wearily. "I sort of doubt that they will, too. Losing their war chief took the wind out of their sails."

Hammond came out onto the porch as well. "Ryan's dead," he announced. "Lost too much blood, I reckon."

"Anybody else hurt?" Fargo asked.

Hammond shook his head. "We were lucky, damned lucky." The gun in his hand came up and pointed at Fargo. "But your luck just ran out, Fargo. I'll take your gun back now, and that pigsticker, too."

Fargo stiffened in anger. Hammond had made a treacherous move a little quicker than he had expected. "There's no need for that," he said.

"Oh? Are you gonna let me take Porter and force him to tell me what he did with our money? And what about those women? You gonna let us ride away with them?"

Maguire started to turn angrily toward Hammond, as did Terence, but at that moment Bagwell and Lawson stepped out onto the porch and covered them with drawn guns. Face taut with anger, Maguire motioned for Terence to take it easy and not try anything just yet.

"What's the old sayin'?" Hammond asked with an ugly grin. "Out o' the fryin' pan and into the fire?"

He was right about that, Fargo thought. By surviving one deadly danger, the Maguires had just traded it for another.

But as Fargo was calculating the odds of drawing his Colt and killing Hammond, even though the boss outlaw already had the drop on him, a scream came from inside the house. Fargo thought immediately of Colleen—Dewey was still inside, after all—but it was Ava Maguire who burst out onto the porch, a look of terror on her face.

"Porter is gone," she cried, "and he's taken Matt with him!"

124

9

That news stunned everyone, though for different reasons. Hammond let out a blistering curse and said, "Gone? How the hell did he get away?"

Maguire took his wife in his arms as tears ran down Ava's face. "He . . . he hit the one called Dewey with a chair, then grabbed Matt and took him out the back window. He knocked Pat down doing it and . . . and hurt him."

With a roar of anger, Maguire headed into the house. "Pat!" he shouted. "Pat, boy, are you all right?"

Hammond's threats a moment earlier were forgotten now. Once again, the boss outlaw was more concerned with Porter than with anything else.

Everyone crowded into the house after Maguire. Fargo saw that Patrick was sitting on one of the benches at the table while Colleen mopped at a cut on his forehead with a wet rag. Head wounds always bled a lot, so the wound looked pretty messy, but Fargo didn't think it was too bad. Patrick was conscious and alert, and his freckled face was full of anger.

"If I'd had a gun, I would'a shot him!" the boy said. "Darn it, Colleen, quit fussin' over me!"

"Settle down, Pat," his big sister told him. "You're hurt."

"Aw, I just hit my head when that varmint shoved me down. I'll be all right. I wish I'd had a gun."

Dewey sat on one of the ladder-back chairs near the fireplace, his head in his hands. He wasn't bleeding, but he had a swollen welt on his forehead.

Hammond stalked over to him and demanded, "How the hell could you let him get away?"

"I didn't think he'd try anything. He hadn't hardly budged for hours. To tell you the truth, Nate, I thought you busted him up so bad while you were trying to get him to talk that he *couldn't* move very much."

"Well, that'll teach you to think," Hammond snapped. "How many times do I have to tell you that I'm the one who does the thinkin'?" He shook his head in disgust and turned away. "Hell, I don't care if you ride with us anymore. You're no damned good."

Dewey lifted his head and stared in hate at Hammond's back. Hammond didn't see the look, but Fargo did.

Fargo picked up a lantern and strode down the corridor to the rear window. Lifting the lantern so that its light washed over the ground outside the window, he looked out through the open shutters. The ground was hard back here and there had been several of the Paiutes tramping around behind the house over the past couple of days. He thought he could follow Porter's trail anyway.

The same thought must have been going through Hammond's mind, because the outlaw came up behind him and said, "You're supposed to be one o' the best trackers west o' the Mississippi, Fargo. Maybe *the* best. You're gonna help us find Porter."

Fargo nodded. "All right. But you've got to agree to leave the Maguires alone. You won't even come back here once we've gone after Porter."

126

"Damn it, you ain't in no position to be dictatin' terms!"

"I think I am," Fargo said, "unless you want to try to follow Porter's trail without me."

Hammond glared at him and cursed some more, but finally the outlaw said, "All right. We're wastin' time. Let's get after the son of a bitch."

"I'll have to round up some horses first. We don't know how far they're scattered. My Ovaro will come when I call him, though."

Hammond grunted. "You're countin' on a horse."

"Won't be the first time," Fargo said as he turned away from the window.

On his way back through the main room, he paused to put a hand on Maguire's shoulder as the burly stationkeeper sat on the bench with his arm around his wife. "Don't worry, you two," Fargo told them. "I'll bring the boy back to you."

Maguire looked up. "I'd better go with you—"

Fargo shook his head. "No, you're still wounded. It'll be better for you to stay here and look after the rest of your family."

"Terence, then. He can go."

"Let me handle this, Sam," Fargo said, quietly but firmly. "I don't think there's much chance those Paiutes will come back, but just in case they do, you and Terence need to be here to defend the station."

Maguire sighed. "I know you're right, Fargo. It's just hard to step back and let another man take the lead when it's your own boy who's in danger."

"Don't worry. I said I'd bring him back, and I meant it."

"Come on," Hammond snapped. "Every minute we waste is another minute Porter gets farther away from us. Another minute he might hurt that kid, too."

Fargo doubted that the gambler meant to harm Matt. Porter wouldn't have taken the little boy with him if he hadn't intended to use Matt as a hostage in case anybody caught up to him. Matt wasn't worth anything to Porter unless he was alive and in good shape.

Just as Fargo had predicted, the Ovaro came trotting out of the trees in response to a whistle. Fargo swung up bareback, his saddle having been burned up in the barn, and rode up the slope, looking for the Pony Express horses and the mounts that belonged to Hammond and the other outlaws.

The darkness made his search difficult, but over the next hour he found half a dozen horses and drove them back down to the relay station. Hammond was waiting impatiently when Fargo returned.

"Can you follow Porter's tracks at night, or will we have to wait until morning?" Hammond asked.

"Trailing somebody at night is always tricky," Fargo replied. "You run the risk of losing the trail and wasting a lot of time. But if we take a lantern with us, I think I can cut enough sign to keep us going in the right direction. Porter won't have a horse unless he just happens to run across one of the bunch from down here. We'll catch up to him pretty quickly, especially once the sun comes up in the morning."

"You better be right." Hammond glared. "I ain't gonna be happy if he gets away now, after I had him right in the palm o' my hand."

The outlaws had to ride bareback, too, and Bagwell and Lawson weren't happy about it. They climbed on their mounts awkwardly after Fargo rigged hackamores out of rope for the horses.

"Are you goin' or stayin'?" Hammond demanded of Dewey.

The young man glanced at Colleen, who pointedly looked away from him, refusing to meet his gaze. "I reckon I'm going," he said grimly. "I want to get that little boy back."

Fargo knew what Dewey was thinking. He believed that if he helped return Matthew safely, that might change the way Colleen felt about him. Fargo thought the odds of that happening were small, but he supposed Dewey was willing to take that chance.

When everyone was mounted up, Maguire handed a lantern to Fargo and said, "Good luck to you, *amigo*. All our prayers are ridin' with you."

Fargo smiled and nodded. "I can use all the good words with *el Señor Dios* that you care to put in, Sam." He lifted the reins attached to the hackamore fastened around the stallion's nose. "Let's go."

The five men rode around the house to the back, where Fargo shone the lantern light on the ground for a few moments before he was satisfied he had picked out Porter's tracks from the others. All the marks were faint, but the gambler's boots left deeper, differently shaped impressions from those of the Paiutes' moccasins. The occasional small footprint left by Matt helped, too.

With Hammond and the other outlaws following him, Fargo rode slowly up into the foothills at the base of the mountains. Hammond said irritably, "If Porter's up there higher than us, he's liable to see the light o' that lantern and know that we're followin' him."

"He knows that anyway," Fargo pointed out. "You've been following him ever since he double-crossed you, haven't you?"

"Well, yeah, I reckon we have."

"So be quiet and let me concentrate on what I'm doing."

Fargo could feel Hammond's angry gaze burning into his back, but he ignored it and rode on. Tracking at night like this was truly one of the most difficult things a man could attempt.

Since he didn't have a saddle and had to handle the

lantern, too, Fargo had been forced to leave his Henry behind at the station. He had reloaded his Colt before setting out on this quest, however, and filled all the loops on his shell belt. He hoped that would be enough ammunition. It ought to be, he told himself. After all, the threat from the Paiutes was over, and Porter was only one man.

The trail rose higher and higher. Porter wasn't headed straight for Black Rock Pass, but Fargo began to get the sense that the gambler was working his way in that general direction. Originally, Porter had come through the pass heading from east to west, and now he was doubling back on that course, maybe hoping to throw off pursuit that way. It wasn't going to work.

In the foothills, the trail was fairly easy to follow. The higher they climbed toward the pass, however, the rockier the ground became. Fargo had difficulty spotting the overturned pebbles, the faint scrape marks on stone, and all the other little indications that told him Porter and Matt had passed this way.

"How come you're slowin' down?" Hammond asked angrily. "Porter could be gettin' away from us, damn it!"

"Unless you want to lose the trail completely, I'd suggest letting me go at my own pace," Fargo said. "This isn't easy, you know."

"I don't give a damn how hard it is. Just find that bastard." Hammond's face contorted in a snarl. "And when I get my hands on him this time, I ain't gonna stop until he tells me where he hid my money!"

"Our money," Bagwell said.

"Yeah, yeah, our money." Hammond jerked a hand. "Just a manner o' speakin'."

But it was an important manner, Fargo reflected. If he was Bagwell or Lawson, he wasn't sure he would fully trust Hammond.

A few minutes later he reined the Ovaro to a halt.

"What's wrong?" Hammond asked. "Why ain't we movin'?"

"Because I'm not sure which way we should go," Fargo said. "I *think* Porter is headed for the pass, but I don't know that for certain. Maybe he plans to veer off in another direction."

"Well, which way do his tracks go?"

Fargo grunted. "That's just it. This stretch of ground is solid rock. There aren't any tracks."

"He's got to have left some sign. What do we do now?"

Fargo glanced at the sky. "It'll be light in another couple of hours. We could wait until then, and it would probably be easier to pick up the trail."

"Wait?" Hammond sounded like he didn't care for that idea. "That just gives Porter more time to get ahead of us."

"Yes, but—" Fargo stopped suddenly as something caught his eye. He said, "Wait a minute," and swung down from the stallion's back. Leading the Ovaro, he walked across the stony ground for twenty feet or so and then stopped again. Placing the lantern at his feet, he picked up something else.

"What the hell is that?" asked Hammond, who had followed Fargo.

The Trailsman turned and extended his hand. Lying on the palm was a small wooden figure about four inches long, whittled roughly into the shape of a man.

"One of Matt's toys," he said. "He must've had it in his pocket and dropped it here without Porter noticing, in hopes that somebody following them would find it."

Hammond frowned. "You really think the kid's that smart?"

"I think it's a good enough chance that I'm going to keep heading in this direction and see if I find anything else he's dropped."

Sure enough, after a couple of hundred yards, Fargo found another of the carved wooden figurines. He hoped that Matt had had a whole pocket full of the little men.

"You were right," Hammond said. "The little son of a bitch is leavin' us a trail."

With the help of the figurines left behind by Matt, Fargo was able to track the fugitive gambler and his prisoner across the rocky stretch. He found three more of the toys over the next hour. By then the sky in the east was beginning to turn gray with the approach of dawn.

"They're heading straighter toward the pass now," Fargo commented as he and Hammond and the others rode higher into the range of rugged mountains. "I'm not sure where he intends to go from there. Maybe over east to Fillmore. There's a stage line that runs through there."

"He don't have any money to buy a ticket on the stage," Hammond said. "I took what little cash he had on him."

"All he'd have to do to get hold of some money is to find a poker game," Fargo pointed out. "Fillmore's mostly a Mormon town, but there might be a few gentiles around who'd be interested in playing."

"Yeah, but he's got that kid with him, too. How's he gonna stop the kid from makin' a racket and yellin' for the law?"

Fargo had already thought about that, and the conclusion he had reached put a bleak look on his face. They had to catch up to Porter before the gambler neared civilization again, otherwise Porter would probably kill Matt to keep the boy from revealing the truth.

"Let's just make for the pass," Fargo said. "Maybe we can find them before they get through it."

They pushed the horses faster, but it wasn't easy

going. Traveling on foot the way he and Matt were, Porter had been able to avoid the main trail and follow a route that was difficult for horses. Several times Fargo and the others had to detour around obstacles and avoid slopes that could have been negotiated on foot.

But they were getting closer to the pass all the time. Fargo could see it now, the notch in the mountains silhouetted by the lightening sky behind it. Since the Ovaro was stronger and more sure-footed than the other horses, Fargo gradually began to pull ahead of the outlaws. Hammond called, "Slow down, damn it!"

"Thought you wanted to catch him," Fargo said over his shoulder.

"I don't want you gettin' there first! I mean it, Fargo, slow down or I'll shoot!"

Fargo looked back again, and saw that Hammond had filled his hand. Fargo pulled back on the reins and brought the Ovaro down to a pace that allowed Hammond to catch up. Dewey did, too, but Bagwell and Lawson were still hanging back a hundred yards or so.

Fargo didn't have any illusions about Hammond's plans. He figured that the outlaw intended to return to the relay station no matter what he had promised to the contrary. Hammond still lusted after Ava Maguire, and he wasn't the sort of man who liked being denied whatever he wanted. But the first order of business was to make sure Matthew was safe, then deal with the threat of Hammond.

They topped a rise and saw the main trail about fifty yards in front of them. And where that trail twisted up into the pass itself, two figures, one small, one larger, could be seen hurrying along. Porter had hold of Matt's hand and was dragging him.

Hammond saw them at the same moment as Fargo did. "There they are!" he shouted triumphantly. He spurred his horse toward the trail, calling to the others, "Come on!"

Fargo was right behind him. The Ovaro could have overtaken Hammond's mount without any trouble, but there was no room on the narrow path for the two horses to run side by side. Fargo had to wait until they reached the main trail to make his move. Then he sent the stallion spurting up alongside Hammond.

"Damn you, Fargo!" Hammond cried. "I don't need you anymore!"

With that he swung his gun up and fired, the blast deafening in the early morning air. Colt flame blossomed in the predawn gloom.

Fargo was expecting just such an attempt on his life. He had known all along that Hammond would try to get rid of him as soon as they caught up to Porter. So even as the outlaw's gun roared, Fargo dropped the lantern and slipped to the side, clinging to the hackamore with his left hand and keeping his right leg hooked over the stallion's back. He could ride Indian-fashion like that almost as well as the Sioux and the Comanche who had originated the tactic.

At the same time he drew his own Colt with his right hand and fired across the Ovaro's back. Hammond yelled in pain and dropped his gun as Fargo's bullet raked across his forearm.

"Get him!" Hammond bellowed at his companions.

But Bagwell and Lawson were too far back, and Dewey hesitated. Hammond cursed bitterly as he reined in and leaped off his horse to retrieve the gun he had dropped. He waved an arm over his head and shouted at the others, "Go on! Get Fargo! Get Porter! Move, damn you!"

Bagwell and Lawson thundered past. Dewey still sat his horse where he had reined in. Hammond ignored him and reached for the fallen gun.

A shot rang out. Hammond sprang backward as the

slug kicked up dust in the trail right in front of him. He looked up in amazement and saw the gun in Dewey's hand.

"I told you I wasn't part of the gang anymore, Nate," Dewey said. "I'm going to take that little boy back to his sister, safe and sound. I don't give a damn about the money Porter stole from you."

"You fool," Hammond snarled. "You don't think it'll make any difference, do you? That redheaded bitch will still hate you, no matter what you do!"

Dewey glanced toward the pass. "I've got to try."

"And that's why you're a fool." The hand Hammond had slipped under his coat came out holding a smaller pistol. It cracked spitefully, and Dewey was jolted back as the bullet smacked into his body. Before he could pull the trigger of his own gun, he fell off the horse and thudded to the ground. His revolver slipped out of his grasp.

Hammond picked up the .45 he had dropped a moment earlier, gave Dewey's body a scornful glance, and then caught hold of his horse's hackamore and vaulted onto the animal's back. He kicked it into a run and went after Bagwell and Lawson as they pursued Fargo.

Up ahead, the stallion was still running well ahead of the others. There was enough light scattered around now for Fargo to be able to see Porter and Matthew about a hundred yards ahead of him, making their way through the pass. There was nowhere for the gambler to hide once he had started through the cut in the mountains. He dragged Matt with him and was moving so fast that the little boy's feet barely touched the ground as he struggled to keep up.

Porter must have realized that he wasn't going to get away. He hauled up short and twisted around, pulling Matt in front of him. Fargo reined in and brought the Ovaro to a skidding halt as he saw that

Porter had looped an arm around the little boy's throat and was holding something that glittered to the tightly drawn skin.

"Stay back!" Porter shouted in a ragged voice. "Stay back or I'll cut his throat, so help me God!"

"God's not going to help you murder that little boy, Porter," Fargo said. He heard horses coming to a stop behind him and knew that at least some of the owlhoots had arrived, but he didn't look around at them. He kept all his attention focused on Porter.

The gambler didn't have his pocket pistol anymore. Hammond had taken that away from him a long time earlier. But he must have had the small knife hidden somewhere on him that Hammond had missed in his search. The blade was only about four inches long— the same length as those little toy figures Matt had used to help Fargo and the others find them—but it looked plenty sharp as it shone in the growing light.

"You know that threatening the boy isn't going to stop Hammond," Fargo said in a quiet, intense voice. "Turn Matt loose, and I'll do what I can for you, Porter."

The gambler laughed harshly. "You mean you'll let Hammond have me so that he can torture me some more! You sure as hell didn't stop him before!"

"There was nothing I could do then."

From behind Fargo, Hammond said, "There's nothing you can do now, Fargo. Step aside, or the boys and I will shoot right through you."

Fargo glanced back. "You can't kill Porter. He hasn't told you want you want to know yet."

"I can blast some holes in him that won't kill him right away," Hammond threatened. "But I don't have to worry about not killin' *you*."

Porter laughed again. "You see, Fargo, you're right between a rock and a hard place. The only way you can save the boy is by saving me. And the only way you can do that is to kill Hammond!"

Fargo stiffened, knowing that Porter was right. And Hammond knew it, too. He shouted, "Kill him! Kill Fargo!"

Even as Fargo spun desperately, dropping into a crouch and bringing up the gun in his hand, he heard shots ring out and expected to feel bullets smashing into his body. But someone else suddenly cried out in pain, and as Fargo dropped to a knee he saw Bagwell and Lawson pitching forward, looks of surprise and pain etched on their faces. They dropped their guns without firing.

Hammond had twisted half-around in shock as someone opened fire on him and the other two outlaws from behind. Fargo saw Dewey stumbling up the trail toward them. The front of his shirt was sodden with blood, but he had his gun in his hand and was still pulling the trigger. The hammer clicked on empty chambers now, though. He had emptied the gun into Bagwell and Lawson.

That left Fargo facing Hammond, and as the outlaw leader shouted in rage, he yanked the barrel of his gun toward the Trailsman and pulled the trigger. Fargo's Colt roared and bucked in his hand in the same heartbeat. Flame geysered from the muzzles of both guns.

Fargo felt as much as heard the wind-rip of Hammond's bullet past his ear. His own shot was more accurate. The slug drove into Hammond's chest and rocked him backward. The almost sheer wall of the pass was close behind the outlaw. He caught himself against it and braced himself with one hand while he struggled to lift his gun for another shot at Fargo.

Hammond never got the chance to squeeze the trigger again. Fargo fired twice more. The shots slammed

Hammond back against the rocky wall. He bounced off it and fell facedown in the trail through the pass. A shudder went through his body, and then he lay still.

"Well, son of a bitch," Porter said in an awed voice. "I didn't really think you could do it."

Fargo straightened and looked at Dewey, who had fallen in the trail behind the two outlaws he had killed. "I had a lot of help," Fargo said.

"I appreciate it," Porter said, and something in the gambler's voice made Fargo turn slowly toward him. "But I'm going to ride away from here now, and you're going to let me. That is, if you don't want this boy to die."

Porter pressed the blade a little harder to Matt's throat, and the boy whimpered in pain as a little drop of blood trickled down his neck from the wound it made.

10

"Take it easy, Porter," Fargo said tautly. "There's no need for anybody to get hurt now."

"I've heard about you, Fargo. You're the sort who'd like to turn me over to the law, just because I once rode with Hammond and his gang."

"Were you part of the raids on those wagon trains down along the Santa Fe Trail?"

Porter frowned. "So you know about all that, do you?"

"I recognized Hammond. I was in Santa Fe a few years ago when everybody suspected that he was behind the gang responsible for looting those wagons. Nobody could prove it, though."

"That's because Nate was slick, damn his eyes. I'll give him that much. But he wasn't slick enough to keep me from waltzing off with nearly all of his loot."

"Why didn't you just tell him where it was? Money's not worth what he put you through."

Porter laughed again, and this time there was a high, almost hysterical edge to it. "Why didn't I tell him? Because I couldn't! I lost all that loot when I ran into somebody even trickier at cards than I am. Hammond's been chasing phantoms all this time and didn't even know it!"

Fargo could only stare at the gambler. All for nothing, he thought. Nothing but hollow vengeance . . .

"Let the boy go," he said. "You want a horse, take it. I won't stop you."

Porter frowned. "You mean that?"

"You've got my word on it."

Porter still looked doubtful, but after a moment he took the knife away from Matthew's throat. Fargo started to breathe a little easier. Porter gave the boy a shove that sent him stumbling forward.

"Everybody says that Skye Fargo is a man of his word," Porter said. "I'll hold you to it."

Fargo went down on one knee and opened his arms. Matt ran to him. Fargo drew the trembling, frightened little boy against him, saying quietly, "It's all right now, Matt. Don't worry. It's all over." He looked up at Porter and added coldly, "Go on, get out of here."

With a grin on his face, the gambler caught one of the horses and swung up on its back. He waved and called sardonically, "So long, Fargo," then sent the horse trotting down the eastern side of the pass.

Matt sniffled, wiped the back of a grimy hand across his nose, and asked, "Are you really gonna let him get away?"

"I told him I would," Fargo said with a nod. "A man keeps his word."

But he hadn't said anything about what might happen if his trail and Porter's ever crossed again . . .

The little cut on Matthew's neck stung painfully but wasn't serious. Fargo checked on Hammond, Bagwell, and Lawson, and made sure that all three of the outlaws were dead. Justice had caught up to them at last for their depredations along the Santa Fe Trail and whatever other crimes they had committed along the way.

Dewey was still alive, though, Fargo was surprised

to discover when he rolled the young man onto his back. Matt was surprised, too, and exclaimed, "He ain't dead!" when Dewey's eyelids flickered open.

"The . . . the boy . . ." Dewey whispered.

"He's all right," Fargo told him. "I'll be taking him back to his folks."

"H-Hammond . . . and the others . . ."

"All dead," Fargo said flatly.

Dewey closed his eyes and sighed. "Good." With an obvious effort, he forced his eyes open again and rasped, "T-tell Colleen . . . I wish things . . . had been d-different . . . wish I could've stayed . . . and showed her I'm not . . . not really a b-b-bad man . . ."

His eyes drooped closed as another sigh eased from him, this one long and final. Dewey was gone.

Matt rubbed at his eyes, which were suspiciously shiny in the early morning light. "I reckon he wasn't really too bad, for an outlaw, I mean."

"No," Fargo said. "I reckon not. He just made some mistakes along the way, and in the end he couldn't come back from them." He got to his feet and put a hand on Matt's shoulder. "Come on. Let's take you home."

Fargo was short one horse, so one of the animals had to carry two bodies instead of a single corpse. Fargo thought about leaving the outlaws for scavengers, but he knew that wouldn't sit well with Ava Maguire if she ever heard about it, and to tell the truth, it wouldn't have sat that well with him, either. He loaded up the bodies, lifted Matt onto the Ovaro's back and climbed on behind him, and then headed west out of the pass, dropping toward the flat and the relay station.

As he rode, some instinct alerted him that he was being watched. He turned his head and saw several figures on horseback sitting on a ridge a few hundred yards away. Paiutes, he thought, and he tensed, wondering if they were going to come after him and Matthew.

But then the Indians turned and disappeared from view, and Fargo decided that the truce was holding, at least for a little while longer. Maybe Satonga's death would give Numaga, the Paiute chief who counseled peace, the opportunity to talk some sense into his people.

The entire Maguire family ran out to meet Fargo and Matthew as they rode up to the relay station. Matt squirmed down and ran to his mother, who swept him up into her arms. Ava sobbed in relief as she clutched her son.

Maguire pumped Fargo's hand. "You did it," he said. "I wanted to believe that you could, but the odds seemed so high against you. . . ."

"I had some help evening the odds," Fargo said, echoing what he had told Porter earlier. "Dewey pitched in on my side, like I hoped he might."

Maguire frowned at the young outlaw's body, which was lashed to one of the horses. "But he didn't make it, eh?"

"No," Fargo said. "He didn't make it."

Colleen came forward and said tentatively, "He . . . he really did help you, Skye?"

"He really did," Fargo said with a nod.

"Then he wasn't . . . wasn't an outlaw?"

"Oh, he was an outlaw. But before he died he said he wished he could have shown you that he wasn't a bad man."

"Maybe he wasn't," Colleen said softly. "Maybe I won't remember him that way."

After Ava finally set Matthew down, Patrick looked at his twin brother's neck and asked, "Does it hurt where you got cut?"

"A little," Matt replied. He looked up at his mother

and went on, "Mr. Porter never would have been able to grab me and carry me off, Ma—"

"If we'd only had guns!" the twins said together.

The army showed up a couple of days later, a company of cavalry riding down through the pass and raising a cloud of dust as they came up to the relay station. Fargo, Maguire, and Terence had already cleared away the rubble of the destroyed barn and gotten started building a new one, although they hadn't gotten much done on it yet.

"The Paiute uprising is over," the officer in charge of the troops told Fargo as they sat on the porch of the house and drank cups of Ava's coffee. "Jumping Pony Express riders and raiding relay stations like this one is a lot different than facing well-armed, well-mounted troops. All it took was a few skirmishes before those savages decided to become peaceful again."

Fargo nodded, but he wasn't completely convinced that the Indian trouble was over. Sooner or later, the inevitable conflicts would crop up again.

"Now that we're here," the captain went on, "we've been ordered to help reestablish the Pony Express service. Even though it's only been running for a few months, the public has come to depend on it."

"Sam Maguire will be glad to hear that," Fargo said with a nod. "He's got pouches of both eastbound and westbound mail ready to go as soon as the riders start making their runs again."

"That will be in a very few days," the officer promised. "In fact, I've heard that Russell, Majors, and Waddell actually plan to *increase* the number of runs because of this Indian trouble. They don't appreciate it when anything interferes with their enterprise. In the meanwhile, my men will pitch in and help get the barn here rebuilt."

"That'll be a big help," Fargo said. "It would have taken Sam and Terence and me a good while."

With the troops rolling up their sleeves and helping, it took only a few days to finish the new barn. Fargo had rounded up all the Pony Express horses he could find, and the same day that the barn was completed, several hostlers arrived with even more mounts for the Pony riders. They were followed by an old-timer driving a wagon full of saddles, tack, and other supplies to replace what had been lost. Now that the Paiute trouble was over, Russell, Majors, and Waddell were losing no time in getting the ambitious undertaking known as the Pony Express back on schedule.

That evening, Fargo was alone in the barn, using brush and currycomb on the Ovaro, when a step sounded behind him. He turned and saw Colleen standing there, a smile on her face. She moved her hand in a wave that took in their surroundings and said, "This is a fine new barn, Skye. Have you seen the hayloft?"

"Yeah," Fargo said, "it's full of hay."

"Why don't you show it to me?" Colleen suggested, her eyes twinkling in the gathering shadows of dusk.

Fargo thought about it for a moment and then said, "I reckon that's a fine idea."

This was the first time the two of them had had a chance to be alone together since all that violence had been crammed into a few bloody days. Fargo went up the ladder to the hayloft first, then turned to offer his hand to Colleen and help her into the loft. Without letting go of his hand, she came into his arms and tilted her head up to receive his kiss.

There was something bittersweet about it. Violence and tragedy had brought the two of them together, and those bloody memories would always be with them.

But at a time such as this, the closeness they felt

could hold the memories at bay for a time. Fargo and Colleen both gave themselves over to the moment. His hands roamed skillfully over her body, finally cupping the firm globes of her breasts through her dress.

"Oh, Skye," she murmured against his lips. "Whenever I'm around you, I always feel like I'm wearing too many clothes."

"We can remedy that," Fargo told her with a smile.

"We certainly can." She started tugging at his buckskins, eager to strip them off of him.

Within minutes they had undressed each other and were stretched out on a blanket Fargo had spread over the fresh hay. Colleen's hands boldly explored Fargo's body. She kissed his chest and his belly as she stroked his thickening shaft. He was fully erect by the time she reached his groin. She leaned over him and pressed her lips to the head of the hard pole of male flesh.

Fargo's jaw tightened and his eyes closed in pleasure as Colleen opened her mouth and took the head of his member inside. She closed her lips around it and gently sucked on it as she engulfed more and more of his manhood. Her tongue slid hotly around the crown.

As she continued to lick and suck, Fargo turned her so that she was lying on top of him with her thighs straddling his face. He lifted his head so that his tongue could find the inviting grotto of her sex. His thumbs spread the fleshy folds, opening her to that most intimate of kisses. His tongue flicked again and again against the bud of flesh at the front of her opening. The muscles in her hips and thighs flexed as she pumped her femininity against his face.

Fargo withstood the exquisite torture she was dealing out to him with her mouth for as long as he could. Then, with his hands urgent on her hips, he moved her around so that she was sitting astride him, her sex poised just above his throbbing shaft. Colleen lowered herself onto him with maddening deliberation, taking him inside her inch by heated inch. It seemed to take an eternity before he was fully sheathed within her, but it was an eternity Fargo would have gladly lived over again.

He moved in and out of her in powerful thrusts. Colleen braced herself by resting her hands on his chest. Fargo reached up and cupped and kneaded her full breasts, thumbing the hard nipples as he did so. Colleen's head hung forward so that her thick red hair shielded her face as she panted. Her hips moved faster and faster, and so did Fargo's.

He moved his hands to her hips and held tightly to them as his muscles suddenly bunched and rolled them over on the blanket, so that she was on the bottom now and he was positioned above her and between her wide-spread thighs. With his weight supported on hands and knees, he levered himself deeply into her, launching into the timeless, universal rhythm of man and woman coupling. "God, yes, Skye!" she husked in a low, throaty voice.

There was nothing gentle about their lovemaking now. The tide of passion had surged up so that it overwhelmed both of them and threatened to wash them away. Fargo kept up the hard thrusts until he felt Colleen spasming underneath him. He let go then, surrendering to his own climax and flooding her with the juices that burst from his rock-hard organ.

Their mutual culmination shook them for several long moments before finally ebbing. Fargo started to roll off of her, but Colleen clutched at him and whispered, "No, Skye, stay there. Stay in me for as long as you can."

Again Fargo sensed that bittersweet edge in their joining. Colleen knew as well as he did that the time had come for him to ride on. He had to get to Califor-

146

nia, to that meeting in San Francisco with a potential employer. Fargo wasn't that concerned about the money he might miss out on if he didn't get there in time. It was more a matter of giving his word and wanting to keep it.

So this was probably the last time that he and Colleen would ever be together, and they both knew it. He lay there atop her as she embraced him tightly, and he didn't move until his organ softened enough so that he couldn't stay inside her any longer. He kissed her as he slipped out, and he felt the warm trickle of tears on her cheeks as his lips brushed them.

"Colleen—" he began.

"No, Skye," she said. "You don't have to say anything. I know the sort of man you are. I know you can't stay. But promise me . . . promise me that you'll never forget me."

"I won't forget," Fargo said. "I won't forget you."

And he knew the words he spoke were true. He would never forget Colleen . . . or anything else about the time he had spent in the shadow of Black Rock Pass.

Sometimes things just didn't work out, Fargo reflected as he sat playing poker in the Three Crowns Saloon, on one of the busy streets along San Francisco's Barbary Coast. He had reached California in time to keep his appointment with that prospective employer, but as it turned out the job the man had in mind was one Fargo didn't want to take. That had caused some hard feelings, but Fargo didn't particularly care. He hadn't been in a very good mood ever since he had left the Pony Express relay station.

Something was wrong, something . . . unfinished.

So he had spent several weeks here, playing cards, drinking, occasionally dallying with one of the women who worked in the Barbary Coast saloons, and doing some uncharacteristic brooding. Fargo had never been the sort of man to let the past linger in his mind. He always moved ahead, his eyes fixed on the future.

He would snap out of it sooner or later, he told himself. Until then . . . well, cards, women, and whiskey helped to pass the time, anyway.

The hand in the current game had come down to him and one other player. Fargo met the raise that came to him and then laid down his cards, saying, "I'll call." Three queens looked up from the pasteboards he placed on the table, flanked by a jack and a seven.

The man across the table from Fargo allowed himself a smile. "Three pretty ladies," he said. "Good . . . but not good enough." He placed his own cards faceup on the table in front of him.

Fargo grunted as he saw the three kings. "Pot's yours, *amigo*," he said.

Still smiling, the other man raked in the pile of coins and bills in the middle of the table. "Indeed it is," he said. "And I think that'll do it for me. My pappy taught me to quit while I'm ahead . . . or at least while I'm not too far behind."

Some of the other players around the table objected to the man quitting the game, but not Fargo. He'd been dueling all evening with the handsome man in the black frock coat and fancy vest, and enough was enough.

The man gathered up his winnings, said pleasantly, "Gentlemen," and headed for the bar for a celebratory drink. Fargo was thinking about getting up and calling it a night, too, when a newcomer stepped up to the table and laid a hand on the back of the vacant chair.

"Anyone mind if I join the game?" he asked.

The deep, cultured voice sent a shock of recognition coursing through Fargo, but he steeled himself not to reveal the reaction. Instead of jerking his head up to stare, as was his first impulse, he lifted his gaze slowly to the newcomer.

William Henry Porter looked back at him, dark eyes widening in surprise. The bruises on the gambler's face were gone and the cuts Hammond had inflicted on him during those long hours of torture were healed, but the ugly scars remained.

Porter must have done all right for himself. His clothes were fashionable and expensive. His hands were well manicured again. Fargo smiled at him and said, "Sure, sit down, friend."

Porter hesitated. He looked for a second as if he wanted to turn and bolt out of the Three Crowns, but instead he finally scraped the chair back and settled himself onto it. "What's the game?" he asked.

"Five card draw," Fargo said. "High stakes, no limit."

"Wait a minute," one of the other players said. "That's not what we agreed to."

Fargo nodded toward Porter and said, "That's what this gentleman and I just agreed to."

The other players exchanged startled glances. They were all experienced men and sensed that something out of the ordinary was going on here. They weren't sure if they wanted to be a part of it, either.

"I don't believe I care for five card draw," Porter said. "I'd rather play one hand of showdown."

"All right with me," Fargo said.

One of the other men pushed back his chair. "Count me out," he said.

"Me, too," another player agreed, and one by one they all dropped out and stood up to leave the table before the hand even started.

Fargo gathered up the cards from the previous hand and stacked them neatly with the rest of the deck. "You want to deal, or should I?" he asked.

"You go ahead," Porter told him. "After all, you were here first."

Fargo shuffled the deck, and slid it across the table for Porter to cut. The gambler did so and pushed the cards back to Fargo.

Fargo picked them up and dealt the first card. His eyes remained fixed on Porter as he did so, watching for any telltale indication that the gambler was about to make a move. Porter didn't do anything, though, except reach out to tap a fingernail lightly on the eight of hearts that Fargo dealt to him, faceup.

"I didn't expect to run into you again this soon," Fargo said as he dropped a two of clubs in front of himself.

"Nor I you," Porter responded. His eyes flicked to the jack of hearts Fargo tossed to him.

"You know, when you rode away from Black Rock Pass, I didn't know if our paths would ever cross again, Porter." Fargo dealt himself the ten of diamonds.

"It doesn't matter," Porter said, a hint of smugness in his voice now. "You gave your word."

Fargo sent a card spinning across the table to land faceup in front of Porter. It was the five of hearts.

"Working on a flush," Fargo said. He dealt himself the ten of clubs. "And a pair of tens here."

Porter sounded a little angry as he said again, "You gave your word."

"To let you ride away."

Fargo dealt the gambler the queen of hearts.

"Never said anything about what I'd do if I ever ran into you again."

Fargo turned over the next card and placed it in front of himself. It was the two of spades.

"Two pair here, possible full house, against your possible flush. Maybe you want to call the game off, Porter?"

The gambler's face contorted in a hate-filled snarl. "Deal the cards, damn you," he grated.

Fargo dealt Porter's last card. "Two of hearts," he said softly. "There's your flush."

"And the odds of filling your full house were just cut by a fourth," Porter said as his snarl became a wolfish grin. "I think luck is with me tonight, Fargo."

The Trailsman turned over the last card and dropped it in front of himself.

It was the ten of hearts.

"Or not," Fargo said.

Porter exploded up out of his chair, his arm lifting as a derringer leaped like a striking snake from a spring-loaded holster under the sleeve of his coat.

As blindingly fast as Porter's move was, Fargo was faster. He came up and palmed out his Colt. The heavy revolver roared a split instant before the spiteful crack of the derringer sounded. The bullet from the little gun slammed into the table because Porter was already doubling over from the impact of Fargo's slug tearing into his midsection. Porter lifted his pain-wracked face, mumbled a last curse at Fargo, and then collapsed across the table, scattering the cards. He twitched a time or two and then lay still as his life's blood ran out onto the green felt.

Silence had fallen over the room as Fargo dealt the last cards in the hand, and most of the people in the saloon dived for cover just before the shots rang out. Now they lifted their heads to see what had happened, and saw the big man in buckskins sliding his Colt back into the holster on his hip. The look of contentment, of satisfaction and completion that had been missing earlier from his lake blue eyes was now there. Fargo was at peace with himself again. He turned and walked out of the saloon knowing that there would be no trouble over this killing, not on the wild Barbary Coast, not when everybody in the place had seen Porter go for his gun first.

The Ovaro was tied at a hitch rail outside. Fargo

pulled the reins loose and swung up into the saddle, saying, "Let's go, big fella."

He was ready to leave the city behind and smell some high mountain air again, to hear the music of a cold, fast-flowing stream and to see an eagle wheeling high in an endless blue sky.

Inside the Three Crowns, the frock-coated gambler who had been the evening's big winner still stood at the bar, one of the few men in the place who hadn't hunted a hole when the shooting started. One of the other customers climbed to his feet beside the man in the frock coat, stared at the bloody corpse lying across the poker table, and said in amazement, "All that, and they didn't even bet!"

The man in the frock coat smiled and said, "Oh, yes, they did, friend. They wagered what my pappy would have called the highest stakes of all."

LOOKING FORWARD!

**The following is the opening
section of the next novel in the exciting
Trailsman series from Signet:**

THE TRAILSMAN #303
TERROR TRACKDOWN

*The hot summer of 1861—and a trail
of terror that leads from Montana to
Minnesota.*

The column of twenty troopers and their pack animals
raised more dust than Skye Fargo liked but it could
not be helped. The summer had been dry and the
ground was parched. It was part of the reason Fargo
had stuck to the Yellowstone River since leaving the
geyser country. Without water the soldiers would not
last a week.

Except for Captain Preston and Sergeant Hunmeyer, the troopers were as green as grass. Most were

boys barely old enough to shave. Most were from east of the Mississippi River and had enlisted in the Army to escape the drudgery of farm life or the dull routine of work as a clerk. None had ever been in battle. Few had ever fired a shot at another human being.

They were green, and they were in Fargo's charge, and he would do all he could to ensure that each and every one made it back to Fort Laramie alive.

On this particular morning, Fargo was riding ahead of the column. As their scout, he was responsible for nosing about and being on the watch for anyone or anything that could do the soldiers harm. From his vantage on the crest of a sawtooth ridge, Fargo watched the survey detail parallel the meandering Yellowstone. They were steadily rising toward a pass high on a mountain range that would take them over the range into the next valley.

Finding the pass was foremost on Fargo's mind. He had been through this country before and had used the pass a couple times, but it was still no easy task to locate it amid the heavily timbered slopes and crags, even with the knack he had for recollecting landmarks. That was the secret to being a scout. Some men could tell north from south and east from west just by the sun and the stars, but that was not enough. A scout had to possess a memory for landmarks or he might as well be a blacksmith or a banker.

In the wild it was not like in towns or cities, where streets were named or numbered and all a person had to do was remember which was which. In the wild it might be a bald peak or a lightning-scarred tree or a boulder in the shape of a turtle or some other landmark that meant the difference between getting where one wanted to go and wandering around lost.

In this instance, a jagged cliff high on a timbered

slope brought a smile to Fargo's chiseled features. He said, "There it is." A big man, broad of shoulder and narrow of hip, he wore buckskins, a wide-brimmed white hat caked with so much dust it was more brown than white, and a red bandanna. A Colt was snug in a holster on his right hip. In his boot in an ankle sheath rested an Arkansas toothpick.

Fargo drew rein. He had gone as far as he needed to. He would ride back and tell Captain Preston that if they pushed hard they could be over the pass by nightfall. About to rein around, he happened to glance down. His lake blue eyes narrowed, and he said under his breath, "Damn me for a fool." He had been so intent on the slopes above that he had neglected to notice recent tracks under his very nose. The tracks were of unshod horses moving in single file. A war party, more than likely, not a hunting party, made up of ten warriors. But from which tribe? Fargo wondered. The tracks could not tell him that. To the north dwelled the Blackfeet; to the east were the Sioux. To the south roamed the Crows. Farther west were the northern Shoshone and the Bannocks. Or the warriors might be Gros Ventre or even Ojibway. Of them all, only the Shoshone were outright friendly, the Crows partially so.

It did not bode well. So far Fargo had been able to avoid Indians of any kind, as much for their sake as for the sake of the troupers under his care. He was not a red hater. He did not believe the only good Indian was a dead Indian. Hell, he had lived with Indians on occasion and rated several as among his best friends.

Frowning at the discovery, Fargo gigged the Ovaro down the mountain. He figured the war party had passed that way the evening before, heading west. By now they should have been miles away and of no threat to the boys in blue. But a sense of unease plagued Fargo.

Captain Preston raised an arm and brought the special detail to a halt. A career soldier, he was in his thirties and carried himself much like professional soldiers everywhere: stiffly, efficiently, with that ever-present reserve that marked a military man. Preston was not one of those who treated his men as his personal playthings. He had been on the frontier long enough to know that a single mistake in judgment could get them all killed.

Sergeant Hunmeyer, or the Hun, as everyone called him, was another career solider. Stocky of build, Hunmeyer was immensely strong and disciplined. Captain Preston was in charge but the Hun's will was the glue that held the details together and molded the troopers into a seamless whole. When Hunmeyer relayed an order, the men jumped to obey. He did not suffer fools lightly, yet at the same time he was considerate of the fact his men were inexperienced boys.

"I have good news and not so good news," Fargo announced.

"The not so good news first, then," Captain Preston said. He had a practical bent, and always confronted problems head-on.

Fargo told them about the unshod tracks and mentioned the possible suspects. "If I follow them to their next camp, I can find out which tribe they belong to."

Preston chewed his lower lip, a habit of his when deep in thought. "I would rather you stay with us. Your best guess is good enough for me."

"Either Blackfeet or Bannocks," Fargo said without hesitation.

"Either spells trouble, sir," Sergeant Hunmeyer said

and gazed over his shoulder at the double line of troopers. "I wish we had twice as many men as we do."

"As do I, Sergeant," Captain Preston responded, "but the decision was not mine to make. The colonel figured the fewer of us there are, the better our chances of slipping into these mountains and out again without being seen."

"Let's hope he was right, sir."

Captain Preston sighed. "We have three more sites to check. Let's get on with it. Mr. Fargo, if you would be so kind, stay with us until we are through the pass."

Fargo saw no harm in that. He swung in alongside the officer as the command was given to move out.

After a bit Preston shifted in his saddle and remarked, "It has been weeks since we left Fort Laramie, and in all that time, you haven't once mentioned how you feel about the Army's plan to build new forts."

Fargo shrugged. "It's not anything I have any control over. Whether I like it or not the forts will be built." The region they were passing through was part of a vast, unorganized territory that stretched from the plains to the Canadian border. Thousands of square miles, largely uninhabited by whites. But it would not stay that way. Lured by cheap land or gold or simply the desire to see a new part of the country, the westward tide would not be denied.

Eventually, settlers would stream into the northern Rockies just as they were already pouring into the mountains to the south. When that happened, they would need protecting. The nearest military posts were Fort Laramie and Fort Bridger, and they were not near enough. So the Army had seen fit to send out a special detail under Captain Preston to scout out possible sites for future posts.

Fargo happened to be at Fort Laramie when the order came from Washington, and since he knew the northern mountains better than just about any white man alive, he had been asked to serve as the guide. Now here he was, deep in the dark heart of a land teeming with hostiles, doing his best to see that all of them made it out with their hair attached.

Muttering had broken out among the men, and Fargo could guess why. News of the tracks he had seen was being passed down the line.

"That will be enough chatter back there!" Sergeant Hunmeyer suddenly bellowed. He had a voice that could put the bugling of a bull elk to shame, and he was not averse to using it.

The troopers fell silent, but to Fargo the incident was not a good sign. There had been a lot of such muttering of late. Most stemmed from odd little occurrences that had Captain Preston puzzled and Sergeant Hunmeyer riled. Things like cinches that came loose and pitched riders to the ground or packs coming apart for no reason or personal items that went missing and more.

Just the other night, around the campfire, a private named Barstow mentioned that maybe the patrol was jinxed, and heads had bobbed in agreement.

Fargo did not believe in jinxes. But he could not deny that a lot of strange things had happened, and that it was growing worse the farther they went. Three days ago a trooper had nearly lost his life when, without warning, his mount began to buck like a bronco. The man had been thrown off and narrowly missed having his skull stoved in by a flailing hoof. A burr was found under the trooper's saddle. How it got there was anyone's guess.

As a result of all the goings-on, the men were constantly on edge. They didn't joke and laugh as often as they used to. In the evening they huddled in small groups or sat by themselves, saying little.

Just the night before, Captain Preston had confided to Fargo, "I've never seen anything like this. Morale is low, and there have been a few instances of near insubordination. If this keeps up, I might have to bring a few of the men up on charges when we return to Fort Laramie."

There was little Fargo could do. He knew none of the troopers personally. They tended to keep to themselves, and regarded him as an outsider.

Captain Preston usually called a brief halt at noon to rest the horses but today he deemed it wiser to push on and get through the pass. His decision provoked more muttering.

Fargo was admiring the countryside. Towering peaks, many over ten thousand feet high, reared to the clouds, their slopes mantled in spruce, pine, and fir. Lush meadows rife with colorful wildflowers provided a sunny contrast to the dappled shadows of the heavy timber. Animal sign was everywhere; deer, elk, mountain sheep and mountain goats, wolves, coyotes, foxes, black bears, and grizzlies were but a few of the creatures that thrived there.

To Fargo it was paradise. But to many of the younger troopers, raised in the safety and comfort of civilization, the mountains were alien as the landscape of the moon, and fraught with peril. They were out of their element and they did not like it.

By four o'clock the detail reached the pass, a narrow defile that slashed the mountaintop like a wound left by a giant sword. High rock walls rose on either side, shutting off much of the sunlight.

Fargo was in the lead, his right hand on his hip next

to his Colt. He saw no evidence the war party had been through the pass, nor anyone else, for that matter, for many days. He could breathe a little easier. But not for long, as it turned out. No sooner did he reach the end of the pass than he spied gray tendrils rising from the broad valley far below.

"More Indians, I take it," Captain Preston said after Fargo pointed out the smoke and Preston had brought the column to a halt. "Just what we do not need."

"Want Fargo and me to ride down and take a look, sir?" Sergeant Hunmeyer asked.

"Fargo, yes. But not you, Sergeant. I want you here with me." Preston swiveled and pointed at two troopers. "Barstow! Weaver! Up here on the double!"

Their accoutrements clattering and rattling, the pair trotted up and dutifully saluted.

"You will accompany Mr. Fargo. Obey him as you would obey me. Under no circumstances are you to discharge your carbines or your revolvers," Captain Preston instructed them. "Is that understood?"

Private Barstow frowned. He had a round face speckled with freckles and hair that resembled straw. "Begging the captain's pardon, sir, but what if we are attacked?"

"See to it that you aren't," Captain Preston said, not entirely in jest.

"But if we are, sir," Private Barstow persisted, "surely we have the right to defend ourselves?"

Sergeant Hunmeyer bristled. "How dare you question the judgment of your superior?"

"Now, now," Captain Preston said, wagging a hand. "They are understandably anxious."

"That still doesn't give them the right to balk at an order, sir."

Fargo did not say anything but he agreed with Hunmeyer. In light of the series of minor mishaps and the rising unrest, it was crucial Preston maintain discipline. Without it, the detail would fall apart.

"We meant no disrespect, sir," Private Barstow said sullenly. "We just want to keep our hides in tact, is all."

"As do I," Captain Preston assured him. "So yes, if you are attacked, you may defend yourselves as Fargo deems necessary."

Barstow did not appreciate when he was well off. "We're to do as the scout wants? We can't make up our own minds?"

In a twinkling, Sergeant Hunmeyer had reined next to him and grabbed hold of Barstow's arm. "You will address the captain as *sir*. He is to be treated with respect at all times."

To Fargo's surprise, the young soldier was not cowed.

"Sure, Sergeant, sure."

For a second Fargo thought Hunmeyer would cuff him. Apparently Captain Preston did, too, because he quickly said, "Enough, gentlemen. To answer your question, Private Barstow, yes, you will abide by whatever Mr. Fargo tells you to do."

Fargo would much rather have gone by himself, but since the captain had made an issue of it, he had no choice. A jab of his spurs and the Ovaro started down. He held to a walk, every sense primed. Half an hour went by and they were well into the trees when he glanced back at his two young charges. "Stay alert," he cautioned.

"How can you do this for a living?" Private Barstow unexpectedly asked. "Are you insane?"

"It's a job, like any other," Fargo replied, adding, "No talking from here on down unless I say so."

"Whatever you say, scout," Barstow said with ill-concealed contempt. "But just so you know, if any mangy redskins try to lift our scalps, we're killing as many of the vermin as we can, whether you like it or not."

Fargo drew rein and waited for Private Barstow to come up next to him. "I'm not your captain," he said.

"What's that supposed to mean?"

"When I tell you not to talk, I mean it." Fargo drew his Colt as he spoke and slammed the barrel against Barstow's temple with enough force to cause the private to reel in the saddle but not hard enough to knock him out.

Private Weaver was a statue, his mouth agape in disbelief.

"Have anything else to say?" Fargo demanded.

His eyes fiery pits of spite, Barstow motioned that he did not.

"Keep it that way." Fargo twirled the Colt into its holster and flicked his reins. He had made an enemy but he didn't care. Barstow had to learn to obey or he might get them killed. Besides, Fargo doubted the hothead would be jackass enough to shoot him in the back. But hardly had the thought crossed his mind than he heard the sharp click of a gun hammer.

No other series has this much historical action!
THE TRAILSMAN

SIGNET

Charles G. West

**"RARELY HAS AN AUTHOR PAINTED THE
GREAT AMERICAN WEST IN STROKES SO
BOLD, VIVID AND TRUE."
—RALPH COMPTON**

OUTLAW

0-451-21868-X

SOME MEN CHOSE TO LIVE
OUTSIDE THE LAW.

Matt Slaughter and his older brother joined the
Confederacy only when war came to the
Shenandoah Valley. But with the cause lost, they
desert for home—only to find that swindlers have
taken their farm. When his brother accidentally kills
a Union officer, Matt takes the blame. Facing a
sham trial and a noose, he escapes to the West,
living as an outlaw who neither kills for pleasure nor
steals for profit. But there are other men who are
cold-blooded and have no such scruples...

Available wherever books are sold or at
penguin.com